A PATIO WITH DIAMONDS

FERAL SHORTS

by

DORSEY

To Martha, Skyler, Peter, Lily, me,
my grandkids, family and friends;
to everybody who has made it
as far as they have.

It is easy to sit in the sunshine
And talk to the man in the shade;
It is easy to float in a well-trimmed boat,
And point out the places to wade.

ELLA WHEELER WILCOX

Words are like leaves, and where they most abound,
Much fruit of sense beneath is rarely found.

ALEXANDER POPE

Improvement makes straight roads,
but crooked roads without improvements,
are roads of genius.

WILLIAM BLAKE

CONTENTS

INTRIGUE:

A MEXICAN DÚO

A Patio With Diamonds

Third person

Written in:

Puerto Escondido, Mexico

Wolfram Darcy's tranquil routine has been disrupted by an imminent and menacing threat, that real or not, he is unprepared for.

He has molded a simple existence here in Oaxaca, Mexico, living off a paltry monthly social security payment he earned driving city buses through the bowels of Philadelphia for the majority of his adult life. He has followed a daily regiment, like etchings in stone, a cognitive map that has not changed during his 15 years living in Mexico.

But now this foreboding harbinger has trespassed on his prosaic daily pattern: first coffee at the El Molino with Will, Gary and Armond, long time residents and expats like himself. Next he will pass through the Mercado Juarez to purchase what he and Edgar will eat that day: fresh fruit, chilies, pan, a cow's head, or bones from a rendered pig, then on his way home down Calle Miguel Cabrera he will buy 'The Independent', an English newspaper he will read between naps. Later in the afternoon, as shadows stretch across his patio, longtime friend, Bob Pumble will drop by with a bottle of Mezcal and they will chat into the evening.

That's about it. Things don't change for Wolfram much day to day, except on Saturdays, when he catches the collective bus out to Pueblo San Tlaxtlan for the always festive market where he will sit on a bench in the plaza listening to the mariachi music and watch the families stroll by. He takes particular interest in the old men, how they have adapted to the pains life has dealt them and how they find enjoyment in the simplest pleasures like watching the children or sipping pulque.

The anxieties of this new concern have Wolfram thinking more about abrupt and violent events and less about the gradual 'demise' that has demanded more of his casual thought these past few years. Having watched the old hippies of Oaxaca, his mentors of easy living, fade into debility and death has him wondering how the remainder of his life will play out.

He has always avoided mirrors, in fact has none in his dark little home. He knows by observing the aging gringos who, like himself, are here because here they can afford to live out their 'Demise' in the sunshine. The yearly loss of muscle mass has left him stringy and leather-skinned. His gray hair, still tied back into a ponytail, is thinning on top and he is forced to wear a hat to protect his exposed pate from the sun. He has exactly three shirt; colorful, short-sleeved and secondhand. He never wears shorts, like some of his expat friends, feels they would draw uninvited attention to him and with these new worries for his personal safety, attention is not what he wants more of. In fact, less is more, has always been his mantra; possibly a rationalization as much as a philosophy. Wolfram doesn't wear jewelry, he doesn't have art hanging on his walls, or pottery adorning his patio, but he has over the years accumulated hundreds of plants, potted in buckets, found ceramic vessels and colorful plastic wash tubs. Plants have transformed his rooftop patio into a jardin attracting birds and butterflies. The patio is really where he spends most of his time.

He has by no intentional or malicious behavior of his own made an enemy out of a rich and violent man who he has never met, and up until recently, never heard of. With his address known to this adversary, his house, which has always been his sanctuary of peace and retreat, has become possibly the most dangerous place for him to be. His house, an afterthought really, is a tiny cinderblock space, pasted on top of a small, walled compound of buildings housing a mechanic shop, storage warehouse and a wool rug weaver's studio.

Hugo Salinas, a fat, complaining man and his landlord, runs the mechanic shop at the front of the compound. Wolfram avoids Salinas as much as possible, slipping out the gate, which sits directly in front of the open shop door, and waiting until he hears a machine so he knows Salinas is busy. If Salinas intercepts him, he will waddle out to gripe in rapid and nasal Spanish about how little rent Wolfram pays, how Edgar harasses Benito, his dog, how hard he has to work....and so on and so on. Salinas usually backs Wolfram up to the wall, his horrendous hygiene demanding Wolfram hold his breath.

Salinas, who doesn't have full control of his whopping, gelatinous body, is stained in grease, head to toe, and his withering, anti-ballistic breath a result of his habit of nibbling on Serrano chilies all day makes Wolfram's eyes water.

Immediately below Wolfram's house is the studio of Telefano Polantentes. Telefan-o-Telly— to his acquaintances—a timid soft-spoken man and Wolfram's friend, has for years been willing to sit and listen to Wolfram's horrific Spanish, laughing with him at his cultural follies and providing him with valuable tips for successfully living in Mexico.

Their relationship is indeed symbiotic, as Telly has found in Wolfram a confidant outside his community he can share his unusual and androcentric ideas with. In slow, simple Spanish, so Wolfram can understand it, he explains how his ancestors, the Zapoteca, were delivered here from outer space, to teach the lowly human contingent of the earth about medicine and religion, and that in the near future all Zapoteca people will be recalled to their promised land, to live celestial and eternal lives, while the rest of the Earth's humans will be tested about what they have learned. Telly thinks that Wolfram won't have to experience this rapturous exit and the disastrous decline that will certainly follow, because he will probably be dead by then.

The repetitive chunka, chunka chunka of Telly's loom just below his house is a comforting sound for Wolfram, reassuring him that, even with his new vulnerability, Telly is still here and things are as they have been.

Wolfram's house, which he pays a meager $150 American for each month, is no bigger than an American home's bathroom, but it satisfies all of Wolfram's needs: a place to sleep, a small kitchen with a table, to prepare and eat his meals, and a bathroom that leads out back onto a small plant-dense veranda where the solar hot water shower hangs off the sunny roof. This climate provides him with plenty of hot water and the shower looks out on the lovely southern mountains where he can see the silhouette of the ancient ruins of Monte Alban. Wolfram takes many showers.

Crudely constructed of concrete and brick, his house was never intended to be a residence. The ceiling is just high enough for him to stand erect and the floor is unfinished and rough. The only adornment in this dark little hole is one of Telly's beautifully patterned rugs, what he markets as Pies del Camas; foot beds.

Wolfram, a visual fellow, finds this a wonderful image. But Telly, as he slows down with age, is barely eking out a living with his weaving and has begun to implore Wolfram to help him market his rugs in the United States where they will command a much higher price. Wolfram has been resistant, having little desire to return home, but now with this new predicament that he fears might be life threatening, he has reopened the possibility.

The patio extending 25 feet out from Wolfram's humble house, really the roof of Telly's studio below, is the only sweet spot of this whole dirty compound. A jungle of his potted tropical plants, Wolfram spends nearly all his daylight hours in this lush garden sitting in his patio furniture, two stained—once white—plastic chairs he salvaged. There are only two because one guest at a time is Wolfram's patio rule. More than two people in a conversation and there is interruption and competition for the stage. This is a pet peeve of his and nearly as annoying to him as people who ask a question and don't really want to know the answer, using it only as an entry into telling you about themselves.

Wolfram enjoys the apparition that his ratty plastic chairs are indeed his patio furniture. In fact he Likes to introduce himself as Patty O'Furniture, to new gringo acquaintances (he is after all Irish), and thinks of himself as a salvaged plastic chair; free, slightly soiled and expendable.

It is the notion of being expendable that is now troubling Wolfram. He has for years considered the fear of dying as something he has, having reached this age and with so little meaning in his life, become immune to. So he is astonished at how the encumbrance of this new apprehension has placed a stress on his soul and how that stress has manifested itself in such a painful and debilitating manner.

He marvels at how his patio, this oasis of peaceful refuge, sits, unknown to those outside the walls, in the center of this grimy compound. Just below lays the scorched, hard-panned courtyard. Naming this a courtyard stretches the imagination. It is more of a battle field, with large auto parts; engines and transmissions lying dead, having bled their fluids to stain the parched earth.

Wind-whipped rubber and plastic automotive debris fill the corners and miraculously, growing out of this barren necropolis, a surprisingly healthy Jacaranda tree, its spectacular purple blooms exploding like fireworks at the lip of his patio. Two mature bougainvilleas flood the patio with blossoms at the other corner. These and the luxuriant garden he has created transform his otherwise shabby abode into an alluring terrace, delicious as it is beckoning.

Very possibly the most intriguing feature of this patio is Edgar, Corvus corax—the common raven—if we can use the mundanity of 'common' to describe this highly intelligent bird. Edgar is at the same time the source of Wolfram's contingency and his greatest pleasure.

Wolfram found Edgar in only his pinfeathers at the base of a pine tree in the mountains near Ixtlán de Juarez five years ago. The nest had apparently been destroyed by storm or predators. Wolfram raised Edgar and they have become housemates.

Tucked under a large banana tree on Wolfram's patio is Edgar's bathing bowl and security cage, where he goes when there is too much noise, it is raining, or it is time to sleep.

These services provided by Wolfram and the address band on his leg, might qualify Edgar as a pet. But considering ravens as pets might be a stretch as they maintain a level of independence that leave you notice that you are not the fawned after master. More like cats than dogs, ravens don't develop an emotional dependency on humans and are willing to hang around you if you are willing to feed them. But don't expect them to throw themselves under the bus to save your ass.

Although insight may not be a prerequisite of intelligence, it insinuates very clever behavior, and Wolfram is always impressed that Edgar remembers, solves problems and understands gravity. He uses his beak as a tool to pry, kill, manipulate, dig and he is masterful at bombing, dropping objects sometimes as large as oranges, onto Wolfram as he sits on his patio reading.

Wolfram has contended the idea of intelligence in a bird with Bob Pumble, who feels that insight requires consciousness and birds don't qualify. Wolfram pointed out that the capacity to discern value necessitates consciousness and doesn't Edgar bring home coins of various denominations? He continued with the argument that insight is defined as evaluating different choices without trying them first in order to make a decision, and therefore implies consciousness. Wolfram offered an experiment to make his point and tied a tasty piece of chicken onto the end of a three foot long run of Telly's yarn, hung it over the patio wall and tied it off. He and Bob drank their afternoon Mezcal and awaited Edgar's punctual return home at dusk.

Edgar returned at dusk, as expected, with his stolen object of the day; a pair of women's panties. Usually he brings home small shiny objects tucked in his throat pouch; a coin, an earring, a bottle cap (Victoria Beer is his favorite cap), and he hides it somewhere on the patio. Wolfram calls this his caching behavior. Edgar stuffs the panties behind a pot and drags a dead leaf over them. His routine, which is far more rigid than Wolfram's rigid regime, is now to vociferously demand food.

Ravens have a full vocabulary of sounds: rasps, honks, carks, rappings, whines, whistles and sing songs, and although Wolfram is not studied in Corvus corax research, he has, with time and interest, become astute in understanding Edgar's communications.

Wolfram gives him no food and Edgar whines and fusses around his familiar patio until he discovers the chicken on a string. He studies it from the patio wall, assessing any dangers. Wolfram tells Bob that Edgar has never seen this strange hanging business before, and other than occasionally bringing home short pieces of Telly's yarn, and once a necktie, he isn't much interested in ropes or string of any length.

Hunger drives Edgar to act and perching atop the string, he pulls up a section with his beak and put his foot on it, then another and another until the chicken is lying at his feet and he eats it.

"There you are," Wolfram smiles, "no trial and error, just insightful decision making. This is an intelligent bird!"

It is Edgar's routine of stealing and caching that has landed Wolfram in his present dilemma. Although this behavior has caused problems for years with Hugo Salinas. Wolfram frequently has to return nuts and bolts, shiny carburetor parts, gaskets, etc., that Edgar has copped. Salinas' greatest complaint about the bird, however, is that his old sleepy dog, Benito, is constantly harassed by Edgar pulling on his tail, bombing him with rocks and heckling him loudly from a low perch.

It is on a fateful afternoon in February that Wolfram notices Edgar burrowing holes and caching his booty down below in the nasty courtyard rather than on the patio as usual. Wolfram goes down to explore digging wherever he sees Edgar's excavations, rather like clamming, and begins uncovering a treasure trove of glittery objects. He accumulates 300 pesos in various coins, a gold chain, three earrings, none matching, a brass hinge, a 10 mm box end wrench, 5 colorful plastic clothespins, 12 Victoria bottle caps and the object that is to change Wolfram's life: a ring.

It is a man's ring, big and garish; it holds a very large faceted stone surrounded by smaller stones all set in gold. Wolfram thinks diamonds and the he has hit the mother lode, but it could just as easily be costume jewelry and all the glitter just glass.

Edgar is perched on an upended engine watching this plunder of his goods. Wolfram looks up from his greedy grubbing, "Edgar, you thieving bastard, you may have just made me a rich man!"

As he cleans the ring he sees an inscription on the inside too small to read. Using necessary magnification he reads the name, Garcia Aparicio Farias. The name rings familiar, but he is unable to place it and so takes his find to Telly the weaver.

One look at the inscription and Telly repeats the name, "Garcia Aparicio Farias, el rey del casino Mexicana. ¿Donde encontré esta anillo?" He is shaking his head wearing an ominous expression.

What he tells Wolfram is that Garcia Aparicio Farias is the Casino King of Mexico, a corrupt millionaire, wanted in the USA for drug trafficking and a man with an unethical reputation for violence he has used to maintain his status. Rumor has it he killed his own cousin in a dispute over money. He was raised in Oaxaca, and his aging mother still lives in the city in a block-square compound, secure and palatial.

Telly's portent, 'Farias will be coming' has Wolfram filled with terror. Should he get out of here? What then would happen with Edgar? Should he go to Farias and explain, returning the ring? Telly estimates the ring is worth millions American, and Wolfram could live high the rest of his life. Wolfram wants only to live his simple, Oaxaqueño existence, in his oasis in the grime with Edgar. Decisions have always paralyzed Wolfram and so he is left with worry.

After a few days he lets hope seep into the cracks of his contemptible and fragile character. There are no expensive cars staking out the compound, but he still has nightmares of helicopters descending on him as he sits in his patio. His equally pusillanimous buddy, Bob Pumble, like Telly, advises him to take the gold and go. He is reminded that El Pez Gordo, the big fish, as Farias likes to be referred to, can't enter the states. There is a warrant for his arrest, but if Farias suspects Wolfram has the ring, his goons will be on him like maggots on death no matter where he is. He decides he must go to The Big Fish.

But how does one find him? How does one get an audience? Is there any guarantee Farias won't snuff him anyway? This is like running with the bulls to Wolfram. He has no experience or history with making decisions that are so tectonic. The whole business gives him a headache, so he drinks more Mezcal and hopes, like an ostrich, that what he doesn't see doesn't exist.

It is this very evening of Wolfram's denial that Edgar, with a routine as precise as a Swiss watch, does not return to the patio at dusk, like he has for five years. What can this mean? Has he found a mate? Has he fallen prey to a predator? Wolfram reminds himself that Edgar is a wild bird, and there has always been this possibility that he might not return.

Telly, always the disciple of doom, thinks Edgar has gone back to Farias's estate for more glitter. Edgar is, after all, nothing if not an insatiable hoarder, and has likely been captured or killed.

This sets Wolfram into a state of vexation and worry for his personal safety. There is an address band on Edgar's leg; if they suspect him of having stolen the ring they can be here in ten minutes.

Twenty-four hours later and still no Edgar and no violent visitors, Wolfram's cowardice dissipates and he realizes how much he misses Edgar. He thinks what a perfect friend Edgar has been. He makes few demands and provides infinite entertainment, not to mention having brought him home an expensive ring. Wolfram fancies he has been a good friend to Edgar as well; he trapped mice for him, drug home cats splattered on the streets of Oaxaca for him to salvage, and occasionally bought him topopos, the salty potato chips Edgar loves above all other things.

It is dusk the following day as Wolfram and Bob sit drinking their Mezcal on the patio. Wolfram is feeling excitement with the possibility that Edgar may just swoop in out of the darkening sky insisting on something to eat, when he hears Benito, Salinas's dog, setting up a serious barkorama. Hugo opens the big gate and two black Mercedes sedans slink into the tight little courtyard. The windows are tinted as black as the cars themselves. He sees nobody but Hugo, hat grease-stained, overalls covering his gigantic stomach greased-stain, leaning into the first car, his grease-stained hands resting across the open window. Hugo raises his fat, grease-stained arm to point up at the patio and in one—as though choreographed—motion five men step out of the two cars and look to where he and Bob are sitting unseen behind the jungle of potted plants.

Bob excuses himself to the bathroom and says,' before the bullets start flying'. The men, four of them wearing black suits and black hats, and the other, a handsome middle aged man, wearing an expensive looking white silk shirt, amble across the oily earth of the courtyard and look up through the vegetation.

"Hello, Señor Darcy?" the man in the white shirt calls up in perfect unaccented English.

"Maybe."

"Do you know who I am, Senor?"

"Not a clue." Still Wolfram has not exposed himself; remains a voice hidden in the palms.

"I am, of course, disappointed. Don Garcia Aparisio Farias at your gate, Senor."

The name on the ring: the Mexican casino king, the worst possible scenario is visiting upon Wolfram, the very one Telly had predicted, and still Wolfram is surprised. "I still don't know who you are, sir."

"You can't imagine how great my disappointment is now."

"Your English is impeccable. How is that, sir?"

"I am an American, just like you, born in Los Angeles, just like yourself. Will you please come out of hiding that we may speak face to face?"

Wolfram sighs and sets the bottle of Mezcal on the patio. He stands a moment to let the dizzy drain out his pant legs and slips through the verdant wall to appear at the railing.

"There now, you are real after all."

"Real old!"

"I believe you have my ring, Senor."

Wolfram is left with playing dumb now. Like his mother told him, 'Once you tell a lie, you are stuck with defending it'.

"Well, my bird did bring a ring home a week or so ago—he is a raven and loves shiny things."

"That would describe my very expensive diamond ring."

"He is a raven; he does not know 'borrow' from 'buy'. He is a simple creature with an affinity for shiny objects lying around."

"I took my ring off while swimming, Senor, and laid it on the table by the pool. Your crow stole it. I will need to see the ring now, and understand I will be very upset if you don't have it."

"These men with dark glasses make me nervous."

"Yes, Senor Darcy, this nervousness you describe is an advantage I enjoy in conversations."

"My raven is missing. You don't know where he is do you?"

"Yes, I have your crow and he will be released once I have my ring."

"Could you please send him off tomorrow morning so that he can find his way?"

"Of course, Senor. The Ring!"

Wolfram feels the great curtain of worry being drawn open as he enters his house. He shouts to Bob that all is well, the guy is a decent fellow, and he has Edgar and will be releasing him as soon as he has his ring. Bob is gone, shinnied off the shower veranda like a chickenshit kid. Wolfram digs the ring out from under his mattress and puts it in his pocket.

At the bottom of the stairs he looks into Telly's studio and imagines him quaking in the shadows of his loom. As he approaches, the thugs move from behind Farias, seeking, what Wolfram imagines, better shooting positions. He notes two of them unbutton their suit coats.

Handing the ring to Farias, he offers, "How was I to know it was yours? And these stones could be glass as far as I know."

"My name is engraved on the ring, here, difficult not to see. And the ring, Senor, is worth $800,000 US. I am going to overlook this mistake and hope I don't see your crow again!"

"Ravens, sir, are by nature greedy beasts. They take more than they need; they hoard. Even when they have not eaten for days and come upon a bounty, they hide food before they eat. In this way they are like some people you may know; never satisfied with what they have and always wanting more."

"Thank you, Senor Darcy, for that illuminating lecture. I now bid you good afternoon, hopefully goodbye, and pray you remember my name."

Edgar returns home at noon the next day, breaking his life-long and rigorous routine of returning at dusk, hops into his security cage, makes no comedic demands for food, although Wolfram has potato chips and a roadkill anteater waiting for him, and he spends the remainder of the day making quiet, self-calming cluckings.

It is now nearly a week later. Edgar has seemingly put the trauma of his incarceration behind him, and has resumed his schedule of returning at dusk, hungry and bearing gifts.

Wolfram has fallen easily back into his inane existence of waiting for death in the self-indulgent trance of living in the moment. Bob Pumble is back and they relax on the patio sipping their Mescal, enjoying the enhanced visual of Bob's shimmying in fear off the shower veranda and Wolfram surviving by lying to a murderer. And as they are having a laugh at the Don Garcia Aparicio Farias's expense, making light of his pretty-boy silk shirt and greased hair, killing his feeble-minded cousin over a fewbucks in LA and imagining him counting his pocket pesos worrying that the 'crow' has come again, Edgar returns home.

He circles the patio twice, a new precaution he has added to his routine since his adventure, alighting on the railing and puffing out his feathers with harsh rak..rak… rak to express a masculine dominance of place.

From out of his throat pouch, a raven's traveling bag, he regurgitates two nuggets of dog food and a petite diamond ring with a stone big enough to encourage Elizabeth Taylor, dead or alive, to give marriage another chance.

At the sight of the ring Bob is up and heading for his escape route off the veranda, while Wolfram is listening for an approaching Mercedes and scripting his plea for mercy.

Thanks Hoppy

First person

Written in:

Guanajuato, Mexico

 It was in La Cabeza, a dusty pueblo off Federal Highway 29 in the northern state of Coahuila, where darkness overtook my drive to the US border. Driving the roads of Mexico at night is not advised. With no shoulders and darkness it would be difficult to avoid an abandoned vehicle, a large rock left in the road from earlier in the day that was used to warn motorists of an abandoned vehicle, or maybe a suicidal cow. I stopped at the first hotel I came to. The word is the same in all languages, but out here in this rural, god-forsaken state where tourists would never come, hotel is a word seldom seen.

The cockroaches told the whole story as I stepped into my room, but it was a cheap place to sleep, and as soon as I got something to eat, that was exactly what I would be doing.

"La comida"? I ask the squat lady with the 'red sky in the morning' eyebrows at the desk. She is a Mexican Mixta, definitely more Indian than European, and although I pay no heed, those eyebrows tell me of a coming storm. She points me down a narrow, cobbled street that is very dark at the other end with a few bare bulbs illuminating weathered wooden doors with pale, yellow light. There is some place to eat down this street? I am hoping she understood I was looking for food when I said, 'comida'. My bad Spanish spoken with a bad accent, she might have heard 'vomito' and thought I was looking for a place to vomit; I notice others have chosen this alley for that purpose.

Maybe I can get up early tomorrow, drive to the next town and eat, but hunger trumps good judgement every time, and I walk into the shadows of this deserted town. The only door I find open looks into a primitive and dingy kitchen. Without crossing the threshold I lean in and clap my hands and call in a thin-pitched, feminine manner, "¡Hola!"

A leathery grandma in a worn out apron appears from out of the darkness.

"¿Comida?" I ask, accentuating the 'C', my eyes talking as loud as my lips.

She nods and sets about the kitchen working up the flames in the old wood-burning stove, dragging pans out of cupboards as she picks up the thick braid of gray hair off her breast and sets it over her shoulder. She is wearing a pretty flowered dress and her deeply wrinkled skin is the color of coffee. There is beauty in her eyes that tell nothing about what she is thinking.

I'm sitting on the rickety wooden bench just inside the door when a man enters off the dark street. I smell tobacco before I see his face. My eyes rise across the man's new boots and creased jeans, making assessments on their way up. He certainly isn't another barefoot composino in thread-bare, polyester pants I would expect to see in a dusty town like this.

On top of his strong shoulders smiles a hard, middle-aged face. "¡Amigo!" he addresses me as he sits next to me on the bench.

The smiling 'Amigooo!' is not making me feel very safe and warm.

"¿Why here?" His jingling, sharp-edged, rapid delivery melts the English words to almost unrecognizable.

"I came to eat. I am staying in the hotel." I think he is just being friendly. You have me sighted in as naïve, so he certainly has my number.

"¡Ayee!" Too loud, too close, too happy; a yelp from Amigo. Gold tooth glittering, his breath, heavy with Tequila, hurricanes my face. He throws his inebriated arm over my shoulder. I'm smiling back at him like a deaf mute. This is too much good will, and when is that old woman going to have food ready?

I do a little evasive scoot away from him and he locks me down by dropping his really heavy hand on my chest.

"¡Amigo, we go!" He's bonking me on the chest. This is when I realize he's got a revolver in that heavy hand. I smell his face just inches away, while my face is studying that big gun on my chest. I am focusing hard on maintaining a calm countenance right down to the guise of dismissal on my lips.

But, I'm not fooling anybody. The gun is dancing on my chest to the wild syncopation of my heart and my words come out tremulous and high-pitched, "No, thank you, but I can't. I've got to get up early and hit the road."

Second only to asking my high school history teacher what kind of planes they flew in the Civil War, this has to be the dumbest thing I've ever uttered.

The fear that I've been naming as irrational, the one designed by the US State Department and the media about northern Mexico's drug cartels and kidnapping rings, is just now building up a head of steam.

He does his 'Amigo' yell again and laughs out an incredulous, "¡Amigooo!" He encourages me off the bench and out the door. A quick glance over my shoulder and I see that the Senora is not even in the kitchen.

My new friend guides me back toward the hotel. I plead all of the expected questions: whats, whys and wheres, but he either doesn't comprehend my English or he's letting his gun do the talking. When we reach my car, the only one at the hotel, he extends his free hand and demands, "¡llaves!"

I don't have clue what 'llaves' means, but he clearly wants the keys. I point up to the hotel.

As we enter the hotel the silent Senora with the vulture wing eyebrows at the registration desk finds her tongue and unleashes an effusion of harsh sounding words, none of which I understand. He is defensive in his response; this is what I read in his body language, his arms fully engaged in the conversation; the gun flailing about. If I didn't know better I would say these two are married, at least have slept together. I mean why else would she be so aggressive?

It appears I am momentarily forgotten, or indeed I might be the topic of the conversation, but I take advantage and ease up the stairs in hopes of gathering up my keys and passport and escaping.

My amigo, however, is behind me as I enter the room. I toss the pillow over my passport and retrieve my keys from a jacket pocket.

With his arm thrown over my seat, the revolver pointing the way, I drive him deep into the dark, rural Mexican night.

I'm not hysterically scared. Why am I not hysterically scared? I am being kidnapped, at best by a smiling cartel henchman, or whatever kind of violent, malevolent person he is. I think it is the smiling part that has convinced some gullible ninny in my busload of personalities, that he is a good guy and that we are going to a fiesta; maybe there will be a stripper.

So I am just scared; hysterical comes later. Soon we are driving on dusty streets, soft like new snow, through a neighborhood of crappy, little houses, some with dimly lit windows. He signals me to turn into a desperate property with a completely destroyed stone wall, oddly punctuated by a high secure-looking gate.

He reaches over and honks the horn with the barrel of his gun then looks at me with his big, gold-flecked smile having enjoyed the cute noise his gun has made: beep, beep….beep, beep.

We wait. I am beginning to think about escaping; a little late maybe. If he gets out to open the gate I'm speeding away. I'm thinking he'll shoot at me, but I don't see him stopping an escaping car with bullets like they do horses in the movies.

But the gate swings open and standing in its dark void is a big stereotypical Mexican— big boots, big sombrero, big black mustache, big blousey sleeves; just big everything. The headlights bright on his sinister face cast dark cloud shadows off his amazing nose and the push broom covering his upper lip, like ivy clinging to a British castle. A cigar is clenched in his teeth. I got to believe Clint Eastwood at his ugliest might step aside if they were to meet at the toilet door.

Amigo reaches over and honks again then waves him out of the way, mumbling disgustedly in Spanish. Disgust isn't about words; it's about how they are said.

The big Mexican gives a sharp little start, like he is surprised we wish to enter. He moves aside. We drive into a dark, dirt courtyard. I can imagine chickens and pigs appearing out of the open house door during the day to root and scratch about.

An old ratty white Ford pickup is backed up to the door. A confused jumble of furniture comprises its bed. This truck is as Mexican as a bowler is British.

Amigo gets out of my car and starts in on the big Mexican who is just closing the gate. His tone says, 'I think you are a piece of shit' as he directs the big Mexican in whatever's about to happen; something I imagine I am a part of.

He reaches his hand though my window, palm open; he wants something. I give him the Chiclets on the dash and he thrusts his swarthy arm in and removes the keys. "¡Espera!" he commands me. I hope that means sit still because that is what I am doing.

I watch the big Mexican load more chairs and tables onto the truck. He ducks into the cab to turn the music up, bumping his head and knocking the big hat onto his back. He darts an angry glance at me like maybe it is my fault, but I'm not looking, no sir! When this happens again, I am wondering if he's been bumping his head for a long time now.

The Amigo goes into the dark house and I am thinking about making a run for it. Before I make this decision I imagine getting away, hiding in this dark, desperate Mexican village, totally unprepared, and I come up with the only good thing about this scenario: I wouldn't be naked.

Amigo appears out of the darkness to cuff the big Mexican on the back of the head knocking his sombrero onto his face, calling him something like 'Payaso', which if I heard it correctly means clown, and returns to the house. I am now considering the key that's always wired to the bottom of the radiator. Could I slide out and under the front of the car, untwist that key, and get back in the car without being discovered? Maybe so as Payaso, or whatever his name is, doesn't seem to be the quickest player in the league.

My left hand has found the door handle after a half-hearted search, when Amigo busts out of the house in a renewed state of agitation. He shouts "¡Payaso!" and cuffs the big Mexican on the head, knocking his hat onto his face again.

His movements are manic except when he stops for just a second, turns his head my way, points the gun at me and stares me off. I have no plans.

They rearrange the furniture in the back of the truck and bring out a final piece, a long wood cabinet that they stand up at the back of the bed. I can see that even if tied down it is in danger of tipping out, but I figure, whatever is happening in the back of that truck, it is not my business.

Amigo waves me to come. I point at myself with an accompanying surprised expression. He rolls his big head to the side, slightly cock-eyed, like dogs do when they're thinking, "You're kidding me!" I walk to where he and Payaso are standing behind the truck. Outside the car I smell wood smoke and something cooking, maybe a house is burning in the neighborhood. This reminds me I haven't eaten or gone to the bathroom for a long time.

I can see the tall cabinet is a clock with a long door beneath it. The door is open and Amigo is looking at me and pointing to it. I need further instructions. He grabs my arm and urges me to crawl onto the tailgate of the pickup.

Payaso is smiling a dumb-ass smile, glad to be off Amigo's shit list, however temporary. He pushes me toward the clock and I finally catch on that they want me to get in that skinny, dark cabinet.

I hear myself say, "Que the hell!" This is as close as I can get to saying, 'What the hell' in Spanish.

Payaso is up on the tailgate now, pushing me back into the cabinet. I have to scrunch my shoulders, but it is tall enough for me to stand inside. I am in full

English mode. "What d'ya want, money? You want money? What ya doin' with me?"

This is beginning to feel like claustrophobia, my least favorite phobia, the one that was lodged in my psyche when a fourth grade chum shut me in the frigid limited-air of my mother's chest freezer, for thirty seconds during a bosom buddy ritual. Thirty seconds is the half life of an isotope of Krypton when you are inside a freezer.

Payaso kicks my feet into a splay and closes the cabinet door. My nose is touching the door. The panic spreads through me like embarrassment. I feel myself losing control to it, being pulled away from an air source, and I say to myself, "It's in your head!" but my head is not here and I am beginning to hyperventilate.

My feet and hands are jammed so I beat my head on the door, bam, bam, bam, like a woodpecker. I hear the truck start, an unmufflered roar, and I am tipped out of equilibrium as we lurch out of the courtyard. I can hear the music above the roar of the truck. This means it is really loud; it's that accordion and trumpet music Mexican guys listen to gathered around a white Buick with shiny wheels in the Safeway parking lot on Saturday afternoons. Payaso must be driving. This is as much as I can figure, but the reality check has temporarily emancipated me from the terror of claustrophobia.

But, just this realization and I feel it returning, like the crazy catch-22 that when you recognize you are in the moment and suddenly you aren't any more. I can't see it, but I know the door is closed in front of my face and I'm finding it hard to breathe and a cold, windy dread shivers me just like being back in that freezer in the 4th grade.

I am screaming. My screams are lost in the cacophony of the truck and the radio, like a pebble disappears in deep water, but it brings me relief.

My clock cabinet is rocking like a bobblehead now, and the instant it topples I experience a weightlessness, time-expanding, disorientated free-fall that I gasp a breath to.

The touchdown isn't concussive. We've landed on something spongy; a
ditch full of weeds or a field trip of small children. The cabinet is face down,
my arms and legs still trapped. I have to turn my head to breathe. My ears
are ringing, my nose is bleeding, and blood flows down the inside of the
door and into my mouth. It is salty and carries fear into me…real fear, not
checkbook fear, more like death fear.

I do not hear the truck. Payaso doesn't know he has lost his clock. This is it.
This is shit creek!

I shout. It hurts my chest, but it brings help. Somebody is outside my cell. I
hear their feet, feel them rocking the cabinet. I shout again and it's silent. I
likely scared somebody off; an old Catholic woman, maybe, who thinks it's
the voice of God warning her to never waver from the tenets of the church,
like do service for the needy. But she doesn't see anybody in need and flees.

A few moments later I hear footsteps running toward me, feel the cabinet
being rolled over and the door jerks open. Two dirty little kids stare down
at me, my face bloody, arms and legs lifeless, and one can imagine them
thinking I am a corpse in a coffin, and—just like you when you were a kid
and there was a situation you didn't want to be a part of—they run like hell.

I manage to unstuff myself from the clock, figure I'm not waiting around
for Payaso to return and I head down the road in the opposite direction I
thought I heard the truck leaving. I am injured, dizzy, confused, lost, scared,
alone and hungry. Life offers up these defining moments; puberty and old
age; tipping points like heart attacks, vision quests and love; intersections
with clarity. I may be heading in the wrong direction, but whatever direction
I'm heading in it is imperious.

I scuttle along the dark highway, slipping off the road when the occasional
car passes. I see a few lights off in the distant Chihuahuan desert. Everything
hurts, especially my foot, and I dig the hotel key out of my shoe and deposit
it safely in my pants pocket.

Dawn is stealing out of the east when I come to a small pueblo. A few
disconsolate buildings cast bleak silhouettes with one lighted window below
a cantina sign, radiating dim rays of light to wash across two dusty pickups

and my Ford Fiesta. No time for me to watch and decide; there's my car, there is a key stashed under the radiator. B e bold, seize the opportunity. I slink across the street and slide under the car, legs protruding…perfectly susceptible. Stiff fingers untwist the wire holding the key. I understand that hurry is the sole action that works against its definition, but I'm in a big hurry as I fumble in the half light to find the ignition slot.

Now I am barreling out of here, thunder and dust, no money, no passport, less than a quarter tank of gas. With no plan but to clear out, I am earnest and intent. I watch the road in the rear-view mirror to see if I am followed, but nothing vehicular in that town is going to catch me, and I experience sensations of exhilaration, escape, adventure; hunger. Just as quickly I am swamped by reality: I have no money for gas, my map is gone, and the oft offered admonishment plays across my recorder, "Don't stop in northern Mexico, especially border towns. Pass through like the smell of asparagus".

Then the gurgle! What? Notes of angelic burbling and I take a quick inspection of the back seat and see the swaddled infant, bushy eyebrows— no shit—just like the eyebrows of that wicked woman at the hotel, and beady little black eyes looking suspiciously at me, if infant eyes are capable of looking suspicious.

Shit! A baby! In my car. Do the math: no ID, no money, Mexican baby on board: child thief! I imagine they dispense with American kidnappers as quickly as Mexican rustlers were hung.

I can't operate this car and strategize. Slamming on the brakes, the baby rolls onto the floor. I surrender the strategizing and speed off with a wailing baby on the floor of my car, which is the safest place for the kid and as long as it is bawling, I know it is breathing.

How did this baby get in my car anyway? I'm calculating here, and the equation comes out to—Amigo. This is his kid with the raging woman at the hotel and he is drinking the sun up at the cantina while the baby is sleeping off its day in the backseat of my car he had stolen from me. I need to go to the police, immediately. It is the only way out of this, but what police?

This dark road leads me back into La Cabeza. Skidding to a stop outside the hotel I wrestle the baby, which is facedown on the floor, out of the back seat. My intent is to get out of here as quickly as possible. I am going to deposit this baby here where I think it lives, which to my way of thinking is heroic behavior, and trade it in for my passport. I bound upstairs, unlock my room, but the passport is long gone. The Senora, who I have conjured as the baby's mother, steams into the room, sees the baby, and gives a shriek of weep and rushes me. I stiff-arm her, shout, "Mi passaporte!"

I hold out my hand. Her face goes from compassionate, frightened mother to an evil and menacing bitch. This is when she attacks me again. She has the same Frida Kahlo eyebrows as the baby, diving from above her ears to the bridge of her nose.

"Passport!" I demanded again and sidestep her advance and head down the stairs. She is crying frantic and incomprehensible slander. I am heading for the door, a major bluff for me, as she dives into a room under the stairs and returns with my passport. I grab it out of her hand within the same motion of launching the baby toward her.

I'm back on the highway in a flash, documented and heading north!

With every mile I feel more the lucky escapee. It is all rocketing through my head what I've been through, and I am hungry. I crest the rise at a high rate of speed and there sitting perpendicular to the road is a cop car. Well, I'm not looking for cops anymore, so I brake hard and the Fiesta performs the expected squealing, fishtailing, nose dive. I suppose you're only as guilty as you look. He's got me dead to rights, so I blink and slow to pull in next to him, prepared to ask a stupid question like, "Which way to the USA?" thinking he'll feel good about knowing more than a gringo and let me go on my way.

It is when I am nearly stopped that I realize he is just a painted head on a plywood cutout cop car designed to moderate speeders through fear; the only way it can be done.

My eyes glance at the gas gauge every few seconds. I am hoping it is wrong. Watched pots may not boil, but a watched gas gauge moves right on down. My only option here is to trade something for gas. All I've got besides my little backpack with clothes and my new boots is my computer, with all my passwords and security codes in a document right there on the desktop. I reach over and jam it under the passenger seat. It's going to have to be my boots!

By the next town I come to, El Zapato, I've gone from head to shoes, perfect. There is a Pemex gas station, number 36,894. They're all numbered you know. I pull in; the attendant guy hoping for a good propina, rushes to my window.

"Gas." I exclaim. I open the door and point to my boots, "Boots for gas."

He doesn't get it, why should he? I take them off and thrust them into his arms, point to the gas pump and say too loudly, "Trade!"

He's confused, we're all confused, and he points across the street to a little bar with two pickups and a mule out front.

I clomp across the highway in unlaced boots, with absolutely no plan. Desperation has begun to corrode the fringes of my ever-thinning confidence. I'm shaking my head at the recipe for this predicament I am in, with its ingredients of innocence and ignorance, hard-headed inattention, and let's not forget, the dash of stupidity.

My wife and I had driven into Mexico to visit our son, living in Zacatacas in the central highlands. When my wife was compelled to fly back because she didn't feel her aching back could handle a long drive, I saw it as an opportunity for an interesting road trip on a different, less travelled, route back to the states.

My map has disappeared, so I don't know for certain where I am, but I figure I am less than a tank of gas from the border. I don't imagine Amigo is wishing me happy travels right now, and that I'll be seeing him soon if I don't get some gas and skedaddle.

I open the door of the saloon and stand in the portal staring into the blackness waiting for my eyes to adjust. The intense morning sun is right at my back and making me just a silly, obviously NOT Mexican silhouette in that doorway. A target comes to mind, to anyone who might be inside.

As my eyes regulate I can make out two Mexican men, bandits for certain, sitting at one of the three tables. They are drinking Mezcal out of a bottle and as I step in further I can see they are sneering at me out of the smoky darkness. I only imagine I hear them snarling.

I put on my friendliest face and offer, "¿Como estan ustedes?"

I step out of my boots and hold them up as I approach their table, "¿Gasolina?" I heard that word used at the Pemex gas station on our way into Mexico, so I am moderately confident that I am indentifying what I want, and hoping (for there wasn't much that had happened in the past 24 hours that didn't involve some hope) they don't think I am just misnaming my boots.

They say nothing, just look at each other and go back to sopping up menudo out of a bowl with a pile of tortillas.

My eyes must have said something to my stomach because my stomach reminded me how hungry I was.

"¡Need gasolina!" I state again.

Again I get no response. A couple of plywood cutouts, like that cop car. I head back to the door feeling helpless, relieved only that things can't get worse, but while I was having this one-sided conversation things have gotten worse. I look out across the highway and there is Amigo and Payaso's ratty white pickup, without furniture, parked right behind my little Ford Fiesta at the Pemex station.

Shit-o-dear! I turn to the two macho ninnies at the table, "¿Baños?" I ask pointing out the back way.

Nothing. Dumb Bunny and his brother, Deaf Bunny, likely haven't used an inside bathroom during their adulthood. Go piss on a cactus, their non-response says.

I drag my laces out the back door.

Dashing from building to building, through a cemetery of dead cars, a goat pasture, and dusty back yards I work my way to the south end of town. Dogs, a fertility of them, pester me at every hiding place. A sorrier lot of dogs I couldn't invent: pregnant, lame and emaciated. Why so many? Is this just the typical under-neutered and over populated mange of town dogs or are they raising them to eat? I might as well be wearing a homing device; my movement can be easily tracked by the barking. Along with a few dark-eyed, nearly naked children, the goats and dogs are the only animals I see. At the far reaches of this tiny pueblo, where the desert waits patiently to take it back, I sprint across the highway, a short-legged bitch at my heels, rows of pink teats swinging wildly. I tuck in behind an ancient abandoned wood building to catch my breath. My frantic scurrying has convinced me I am taking action, although there is no plan associated with this action.

I search through my pockets in hopes (there I am hoping again) I haven't left my keys in the car. I find them tangled up with my lighter, not that this solves any of the problems I am presently facing. But The GREAT idea of creating a diversion is born from the lighter. It doesn't take long to get that tinder-dry building burning.

I stealthily worked my way north on the east side of town. I learn by locking the dogs in a menacing stare and emitting a threatening growl deep in my throat that I can silence them and they slink off. I slip into a storage shed to take stock, and find myself surrounded by a jumble of worthless junk and one big red gas can. I tip it toward me: it is nearly full!

Leaving the shed, the gas can in tow, I hear voices out on the highway, see the black smoke from my fire, and feel a kinship with William Boyd. Playing the role of Hopalong Cassidy he introduced me to the escape diversion in a TV episode from the 50's. Thanks, Hoppy.

I am not exactly counting my chickens, but I now sense a germinating confidence in my odds for escape. When I reach the back of the Pemex station my cursory inspection tells me nobody is here. I quickly move toward the Fiesta, the lid already off the gas can.

I have poured half the can of gas into the Fiesta when I make two critical discoveries. One is Payaso sleeping in the pickup parked immediately behind me. He doesn't look nearly as big without his sombrero. Never the-less I am wishing the gas would pour faster. The words of some wiseman comes to me, 'You can wish in one hand and shit in the other and see which one fills up first'.

The second discovery is that the gas I am pouring into my car doesn't smell like the gas I usually pour into it. I lean down for a sniff and realize it is diesel I am putting into my poor little Fiesta. I'm not a mechanic or a rocket scientist, but I know this isn't optimal getaway fuel. In fact my car may not get away at all.

Grabbing my passport out of the glove compartment (where I have never kept my gloves) and jamming it deep into my back pocket, I sidle around to the driver's side of the pickup and peer into the cab. The key is in the ignition. I ease myself into the cab and turn the key. Payaso lurches awake to the roar of the old truck, but before he is awake enough to recognize I am not Amigo we are shaking and blustering north down the highway too fast for him to take any action safely.

It is a chess match. We both study the other's disadvantages. He's shouting over the pandemonium. I recognize a couple of words, mierda and cabrón, (I think he is calling me a son of a bitch), but I am only concerned with his hands, both gripping the dash as though they were attached to it.

This is my advantage. He's got a dashboard in his hands, I have the steering wheel in mine. But the wheel is demanding great swings from side to side to keep the truck tracking straight. Difficulty made more difficult by a windshield so fractured with cracks, like a map of Delaware, that everything I see is an approximation.

Payaso obviously has no gun or he would have played that card by now. I am prepared to slap his hand if he goes for the key, but his paralysis very possibly relates to his being subliminally pleased he is moving away from Amigo, especially now that he's let me get away with the truck. Amigo is going be plenty pissed.

"It's okay Payaso. I'm going to give your piece of shit truck back to you."

He is squinting at me out of one eye, his toupe of a mustache cocked into
a sneer. He doesn't know what I'm talking about, which makes me smarter
than he because I know what he is talking about when he says, " Chinga tu
madre!"

I have to believe Amigo is on our trail. What he's driving is a mystery. I have
the truck floored, but it is not moving in any measure as fast as its cri de
coeur would suggest.

A great black cloud of exhaust billows behind us and has begun to
accumulate inside the cab. I have no idea what is behind me or ahead. I am
watching the flat, unpopulated desert bounce past by looking out Payaso's
side window. He is staring out mine. Occasionally our gazes intersect; two
planes in an immense sky, and the chess game seems back on.

The gas gauge either doesn't work, like all other dials of detail on the dash,
or we are about to sputter to a stop, out of gas.

"¿Tienes niños?" I think I have asked him if he has kids.

"Seis". There is nothing enthusiastic about how he responds.

Poor Payaso, dumb as a berry bush, six kids, I'm imagining his potato sack
of a wife, stuck in hag mode, and an angry gangster boss.

But, I've got my own problems, like my Fiesta abandoned in El Zapato with
my computer. My concern-o-meter isn't recording much distress, however.
The old Ford has lots of miles and as soon as the diesel fuel is injected into
that gasoline engine its value plummets to about 25 bucks.

We enter Ciudad Acuna; I follow the signs to Frontera International until
we come to the incredibly long line of cars waiting to be granted passage
into the USA.

I stop the truck at the end of that stalled parade, leave it running and tell
Payaso, "Sorry pal, I have to send you home."

I am out of the truck, disappearing into the crowd of humanity walking
across the border. I rest my hand on my back pocket, reassuring myself that
the passport is there and allowing me to imagine myself in Texas, borrowing
a cell phone to call my wife; her making a hotel and plane reservation for me,
a big plate of food on the table and a hot shower.

DEATH:
YUKON TERRITORIES, CANADA

I Could Not Stop for Death

Written on:

Teslin River

Whitehorse, Canada

In 1964, my father died leaving me a 17 year-old orphan. Free for the first time after an unfortunate childhood; my mother's early death, an alcoholic, abusive father, living in cheap hotels or on the street, I bolted. The military had their greedy sights set on losers like me to fill the ranks of disposable foot soldiers for its expanding Viet Nam War. The lateral degradation of going from one repressive situation to another was unbearable so I quit high school in my final year and headed for Canada.

I entered Canada on the Klondike Trail out of Skagway, Alaska, through the Canadian Yukon Territories to Dawson City. Hiking and canoeing my way into what I imagined a Jack London adventure it imprinted upon me an appreciation for solitude, a love of nature and especially my fascination for the preposterous abundance of this unsettled wilderness.

Whether it was the alluring emptiness of the far North, or my successful integration into living in the wilderness, undocumented and independent, I awarded this place a gravity that draws me back as an old man. It is to this Canadian Yukon of my youth that I am returning to die.

Since Margaret's death two years ago, I have collapsed into an emotional bankruptcy; lost the promise of anything new or magic. My quality of life has decayed into a compost of purposeless vegetation. Now with the prognosis of nephritis, carrying a tag line of terminal, I have concluded it is time to live up to the promise I have made to myself and rid the world of another sundowner taking up oxygen.

My children understand my intention and have condemned it as illegal and against the will of their god. In Hamlet, Polonius offers the advice: 'To thine own self be true', so I've taken all the crayons out of my box; I've stopped caring about anybody, even myself. With what little control I have left after my terminal diagnosis, I am taking myself out of the parade. Natural laws trump man's religion and his interpretations and I am learning to accept death with intelligence, not fear. As I think, so I become.

That early Canadian adventure taught me that nobody had authority over me unless I allowed it. It also taught me that alone I was not going to survive the Yukon winter. I returned to the states where my self-authority was expropriated by the US Army when they found me applying for USDA food stamps and they nabbed me.

I went into acquiescent mode; a resignation of will. The kernel of aggression supposedly at the center of every young man's flower had been pulverized by my father's angry bile. I had no intention of violence and decided to answer only to my own authority. The only thing that kept me sane and alive was that I expected to die.

The crisis of the children in the Viet Nam war was my polestar; the hungry, frightened children whose lives had been raped because of the immorality my country embraced in the name of a lie. Passing out my weekly chocolate ration was the only positive I tendered in all those war years.

Along with 2nd lieutenant, Qvus Washington, I was court-martialed for insubordination when we refused to incinerate a village of women, children and old men that our captain 'had a feeling' was harboring Cong soldiers. The court-martial was withdrawn because I was the only one in our platoon willing to walk the mined patty roads ahead of the others. I told them I accept the court-martial reversal only if 2nd Lieutenant Washington, who had negotiated on my behalf many times, was off the hook too. After two tours I left Nam unscathed, the only one in my company without at least shrapnel in the ass. Washington was dead.

Death is my design, the details I leave to fate. In September I buy an over-the-hill Volkswagen van and insinuating myself into an inconspicuous self-reliance, I drive the thousands of miles north toward my intention. The van is old and runs poorly, with bad tires and worse brakes. This nonchalance and its liberating absence of consideration oblige me in my ambition and the careless disregard for details becomes a covenant. I sleep wherever I stop and eat out of the same unwashed bowl each day.

In Whitehorse, Yukon Territories, I rent a canoe from a low center of gravity guy with thick hands; a hard winter type with that charming Canadian affectation of speech….ayes and oos.

"You don't seem especially excited aboot this, Bub."

"What's to be excited about?"

"Well, let's just say you better kickstart your excitement if you intend to do this river solo this close to winter. There is a lot of bad juju that can come calling oot there in the wilderness if you aren't at full attention, aye?"

Good, I'm thinking; death is what I seek. Some things are within our control, some things are not; it is only after you have squared up with this fundamental rule of the Epictetus Creed and learn to distinguish between what you can and can't control that inner peace is possible. Admonishing me again and again that it is too late in the season to float the Big Salmon River, he sends me on my way to The Quiet Lakes and the river's headwater. I find my way there, deep in the empty wilderness and leave the van with no arrangements for a shuttle to be run; keys in the ignition, life preserver and my credit card on the front seat.

I paddle until the sun sets, then on through the luminous darkness of the lengthening Yukon night and out into the full bloom of morning. Pushing on across the three lakes that feed the Big Salmon River, I ignore my fatigue, I ignore the sciatica that has tormented my hips for years, I ignore the worn-out rotor cup that makes sleeping almost impossible and a right toe inflamed with gout.

I put my head down, close my eyes and work against the pain—my body my mind's oxen. Songs of past consequence fill the space my will to live has left hollow;habitual acts of calming the cat. I sing Kristopherson lyrics to the cadence of my paddling, 'I'd give all my tomorrows for a single yesterday'.

I examine the mystery of whether my life is an end in itself or whether there is something beyond it. Does everyone expect to retain continuity, if only in memory, from one world to the next? Could immortality be in the here and now, not the hereafter? These are the silly sentimentalities that string us along when it is time to jump off the train. Is this brooding making it easier to satisfy my goal here or does it drive me back to the desperation of my dependency?

After the war, surprised to be alive, no blueprint or road map, I married out of lust. I failed at every attempt at legitimate profit, so returned to playing music supported by small drug deals. My young children were acquaintances; my wife a stranger. As I viewed this reality through the fog of my detachment I convinced her to take a family vacation to a cabin on a remote river in Eastern Washington State. When she fell, striking her head on the rocks and slid unconscious into the river, I turned away feeling something like satisfaction.

I began my career as the single parent of my children. It was the true north of this unintended responsibility that tendered me a clear view of my compass needle pointing toward children. Working convenient stores at night, raising my kids and going to school during the day, I earned my teaching certificate and the only career that could have saved me from myself. Then I met Margaret. We married and combined our families. What such a beautiful person saw in a soft, frightened, tree-hugger like me I couldn't digest. Gentle eclipses all other traits a man might possess, she explained. So began my resurrection—the 25 years I regard as my history. I found myself, became as whole as I could be under her loving umbrella. When she died I fractured.

Reverie and my regrets bully me into a stupor and I awake hours later, cold and in pain. I have funneled out of the lake into river, flowing strong through the stunning northern wilderness on its way to its mother river, the Yukon. Addling to the shore I unfurl my aching body and I am lit upon by Arctic mosquitoes, voracious with a last chance appetite to get their life cycles spun in the short time available. Sprawling on the soft, mossy carpet of the forest, looking up into the late autumn boreal spindle of black spruce, the mosquitoes, little electric drills, swarm over me and I give myself to them; nothing short of a siege on the essential store of life. Pain is inevitable, I reason, but suffering is optional.

Back in the boat I float at the whim of the river; it hurts too much to paddle. When my water is gone, I drink from the river. I laugh at my hesitation when I consider Giardia and Hepatitis. The words of Ella Wheeler Wilcox rise from my musing, " Laugh and world laughs with you, weep and you weep alone, the sad old earth must borrow its mirth, but has trouble enough of its own". Stanzas and lyrics of beloved authors brought an unprejudiced apathy of fatuous numbness to mask the pain and pass the time.

I have no clear picture of how my death will come, but I recalibrate my resolve. How splendid and sad it is here in the absence of hope. I will die here.

I see only one other human on the river; a scruffy bearded fellow in a dented aluminum canoe, an uninhibited parishioner of this unpeopled paradise, suspicious and guarded with his words. He tugs his gloves, doesn't look into my eyes. Liars always look away. He offers only his name, Baba, and this admonition, "I don't know your business here stranger and I don't care a damn, but winter's at hand and you're comin' onto a stretch of the river bad with bears."

I consciously try not to think about anything, but Margaret comes to me, the family when the children were young, my granddaughter, my wasted youth and why I have waited so long to return to the Yukon—'Oh, contrition', you venom of memory. I wish to forget, but can only remember and regret.

When these pernicious thoughts crowd my thresholds I doze for a break from the aspersion. I am awakened by a beaver's slap or a loon hootling and I float, unnoticed, past moose feeding in the shallows. The huge males are in rut, a pre-mating behavior that renders them very aggressive and unpredictable. They stomp and grunt, stage false charges. Despite my intention, fear and natural defensive behavior rule my response in the form of panic. I take little notice of the spectacular, but nearly spent, autumn presentation of color. Some impermeable filter has slammed down cutting me off from my capacity of wonder, incarcerating the full complement of my curiosity; a hopelessness buoyed only by my intention to die.

I wake from one of my naps in the sweat of a fever. Dry heaves and diarrhea drive me to shore. Like a sick dog I tremble on hands and knees. I understand this is payback for drinking river water. The mosquitoes are on me, but I am too weak to resist them; let the bastards have the bad blood. I manage to erect my yellow tent, for what reason I have no exposition; possibly a reflex calling for the security of enclosure that had snuck past my purpose. My numbed dignity lays wrapped in the yellow jaundice of this tent, delirious and miserable, as the soliloquy of my death drones on: "I've been shootin' in the dark too long, when things ain't right, they're wrong!" The Dylan lyric gets jammed in my febrile brain. And things aren't right. Certainly I will die here, but I don't need certainty with such probability.

Crawling out of my tent thirty-six hours later I don't even try to stand. Deliriously I crumple next to the river and rehydrate myself with slugs of river water. "Hair of the dog!" I mutter to the mosquitoes. Dragging myself back to the tent I collapse to wait for death.

I expect to die, so waking the next morning free of fever and feeling stronger I experience a silly giddiness, a tenuous optimism I can't argue against and I give myself up to it.

Walking away from the river and into the woods with no regard for landmarks, I open myself to an awareness of how far away and vast this Yukon Territory is, just as the Yukon opens its aperture wide to invite in the twenty hours of sunlight to perform its magic. In the race for reproduction, autumn is always immediately at the heels of summer. This is the boreal forest of the far north; spruce trees, lichen, mosses and long winters, alpine in everything except elevation. Timberline here is nearly at sea level.

I meander through the forest that is bursting with the intense end of the brief autumn, preparing for the coming snows that will burden it for the next eight months. Wild rose hips and tufts of dry grass peek through jumbles of downed trees, their repose a gesture of reciprocity with the earth. This forest is too remote to have been logged or grazed.

As I walk across the soft, deep carpet of the forest it releases the odor of earth that moss brings to the sky, and as addled as my mind is, a little verse rises in me, abating the strain: "Moss is the carpet, fending Earth's floor, the forest is the living room, the river is the door".

Songs of birds I never see occasionally break the precise silence, the way light touches glass. Breath is to breathing what silence is to circumspection and these reflections emancipate hunger, that medusa of biology. I try not to look at it, but the need for food is greater than my resolve; too strong to swim against and testament to the lust for life. My meager provisions of bread and granola are gone and my will is hoodwinked by appetite.

When I find the dead finch an idea comes upon me like sunshine: undeniable and demanding my full attention. From the small tackle box comes the #2 hook I lash to the finch with fishing line. I paddle for the far shore where the grass growing along its fringes color the horizontal line of the river golden against the vertical surge of spruce. My eyes are directed up the mountains behind, all the way up to the U-shaped valley, blue with glacier and white with winter's first snow.

I send the canoe gliding through the reeds that grow out of the quiet water along the bank. I study the shallows for the long muscular bodies of the northern pike waiting as still as logs for prey to blunder by. Holding the fishing line in my hands—I decided at the last minute to leave my fishing rod in the van—I guide the finch across their ambush.

The line cuts into my hands when the pike strikes. I am pulled to my knees in the canoe. Tucking the line around the yoke of the canoe I bring the fish toward me. Lunging out of the water it struggles savagely through the reeds then under the boat. The line stresses against the gunnel. I think it's certain to snap. Tiring, the pike concedes to the steady pressure and I drag it into the canoe.

Predator teeth are locked around the bird; the hook protrudes through its lip. The fish thrashes at my feet, easily three feet long, the head itself a foot of that, all jaws and teeth. Blue and textured with scales painted randomly of irregular snowflakes the fish's fins and tail are accented red like sunset. I am arrested by its beauty. Remembering a fishing tenet of my father's that fish are paralyzed with pressure on their eyes, I ease my hand along the spine of the convulsing fish, a sensation of cool metal coming to life, and jam my fingers into the eye sockets. I hold it like a bowling ball and it lies still as though asleep.

The physical exertion leaves me exhausted but exhilarated; a measure of pride resides within the surprise of my success. I drag my prize onto a rocky shoal, bewildered now after so much avowable certainty to die that I am confounded by hunger.

Silent as an infection, the bear walks in behind me as I sit at my campfire, a fillet of pike dripping in my hand. I throw the fish in the bear's path. It rises up on its hind legs, massive and lurid above me. I recognize by the broad head and hump across the shoulders that it is a grizzly. My mind labors for the determined composure I would lock into when my father beat me as a child. The bear lowers itself, steps forward and eats the fish. Internally I am irrational, but my body stands paralyzed before the immensity of this creature.

Running, I know, is futile, an invitation to a bear. A long silent voice from youth, uninvited yet imperative, whispers to me of remaining calm and avoiding eye contact. This defiance is the only control I possess and knowing I cannot be broken unless I decided I am broken.

The bear lowers its head, its menacing stare latches onto me. I manage to divert my eyes, feel the welcome of an objective calm spread through me as my muscles relax and fear transitions into submission. I had experienced this a thousand times with my father coming home drunk; maw of brutality settling over me. If he came into my room there was nothing I could do but be ready. And now I am ready.

Haven't I come here to die? Isn't the window of opportunity open? I stare at it, recognize it, but can't overcome the allegiance to preservation that Human Nature has assigned me. I can't escape its gravity.

The bear swings its colossal head side to side, barks something to itself, and as though being overwhelmed with indifference, turns and rumbles casually back into the forest.

When I collect myself the thought that these bullets I have been dodging might be a predestined commission that maybe it is not my duty to die. It isn't an epiphany, it hasn't come suddenly, but the chrysalis bastard of hope and fear, some enduring animation, is reclaiming me.

Another opportunity, however, offers itself up the next day. As I sleep
in my boat, it drifts into a constriction in the river. The water speeds up,
piles upon itself, stumbles over itself in standing waves as the river tries to
compress through a sphincter in the rocks. Large eddies form on both sides
as water turns back on the current. I awake at the instance my boat is pulled
down across a foot deep eddy line. The bow lurches upstream and the canoe
capsizes. It has happened so fast I have no time to react. I am ripped free
from the over-turned canoe by the strong, cold current. I wear no life
preserver; have purposely left it in van. The cold water pulls me along the
eddy line as I wash through a succession of waves. My arms and legs flail,
an instinctive treading of water that I cannot control. A leg extends across
the eddy line and I am drawn into its force; the water working against itself
sucks me to the bottom. Again reflex blocks my brain and my feet push
off the river bed with all there is to offer. Surfacing in the eddy near the
shoreline, I exhale the oxygen-depleted air I have been holding against
my will. Grasping a branch offered out from shore, as though it were a hand
reaching, I pull myself onto the bank. My gear bag, followed by the canoe
and paddle, float thoughtfully through the eddy. I pull them onto shore.
Prostrate, on the bank by the river, I cry like I haven't cried in over 60 years.
How purging. How cleansing. A catharsis that has me questioning whether
I have been saved by fate or have saved myself?

I have been an insomniac for years, so reason it is the physical exertion
that has me sleeping so well. I awake in my cheerful yellow tent feeling sore
but uncommonly refreshed. I think of the soreness as pain with a promise
to recover; greatly preferring it to the life-sentence of aggravated joints.
Allowing a positive seed to germinate in my fallow imagination, I speculate
that the extremes in physical output have rid my joints of arthritis and, the
soreness that replaces it, will be temporary.

I sleep soundly this night awakening only to relieve myself. As I stand
in the chill and counterfeit light of the northern night I hear the cries. A
spooky bawling comes crashing through the forest toward my camp. I have
no experience to help me recognize what it might be: Banshee, bogeyman,
bear? Would I be safest crawling back into my tent? Should I get in the
canoe and paddle off shore?

Overcoming the mutiny of my imagination, I gather control of my

extenuated intention; I have come here to die. And so I stand, right there
next to my yellow tent with my pants down and wait. The breakage and
bellowing comes louder. I hold, my feet obeying their master, and watch a
moose calf erupt out of the trees and into the river in search of its mother.

I have survived a host of challenges. My system has accepted the water and I
am always hungry now, though the bird is providing me with enough pike to
survive. Although my sciatica continues to be an aggravation, my shoulders
and knees are miraculously pain-free and the soreness has begun to dissipate.

An ache of a different sort has taken up residence in me that food and health
can't satisfy. I am lonely.

Loneliness, the great annulment of gratification, more exaggerated than any
I've known since Margaret died, has poured its venom into me, propagating
hallucinations of home that push down on me like guilt.

The convergence of events and sensations has me re-examining my course.
As though I have come to a fulcrum, like the sun at solstice, I am leaning in
an opposite direction. My thoughts are no longer on my desperation, but the
equity in the future. I am not ready to call 'uncle' yet. Tilly, my five year old
Down's-syndrome granddaughter, pulls on me with extraordinary force. We
share compromised futures and therefore a welded bond. She calls me Cup,
I call her Tea and I can't wait to take her camping. Was it a mistake to have
looked for hope outside myself?

As my health improves I become, again as in my youth, deeply captivated by
this Yukon that I suppose to be one of the few remaining uninhabited and
pristine places on this abused planet. I am held in the palm of apprehension
at the unending campaign of survival waged, the bloody crusade of renewal
that Mother Nature breeds into her scheme, and the essential truth that we
are just another of her children fully under the influence of her laws.

I sense that I am again moving toward answers, a future perspective which
brings with it the failure in patience that is necessary to examine what
must be listened to through the silence of believing to understand. If I
can ignore the 'hurry in hopes of something more' and sit in the quiet of
my own footprint, then presumption will grow bored and leave me alone
with discovery. But I also know from my year of living naturally here that

winter comes early to the Canadian Yukon, and it comes hard. Autumn is consuming its condensed allotment rapidly and I fear the angry moods of change about to beset this awesome wilderness. I supposed it is human nature to worship what we fear.

On my seventh day on the river, each is shorter by 20 minutes than the one before as this free-fall into winter takes great gulps of daylight with it each day. A light snow is falling and it is cold; as though I have floated out of autumn and into winter. I ride my boat in the corona of recovery, my hands cupped in my lap for warmth. A universal posture of acceptance, I postulate. The Big Salmon River has indeed become big; corpulent with the smaller streams it has ingested. Deep now, its current still strong but, constricted by the coming confluence with the Yukon. Mother River of the deep north.

I consider where I can get off the river, the difficulties of getting back to my van and how I will manage without money. But these are, I sense, small problems; not problems at all, but opportunities of engagement. I am undaunted. I listen now to my refashioned intention with an alertness that suggests anticipation or satisfaction and laugh out loud at what I have survived; how I had come here to die and now am contemplating returning to this spectacular place in the future. The positive energy mounds over my terminal prognosis like dirt thrown on a grave.

I beach my boat to relieve myself like I have done dozens of times over the past week. Standing in a grove of Aspen, I gaze through their winter nakedness into the cataract of the steel gray sky. It is very cold and my coat is inadequate. I am shivering and yet I smile in celebration of my metamorphosis. I am living now, not dying. This petulant and enduring river has cured me; has purged the poison that has for years accumulated in me. Maybe a divine will does exists and is directing the universe? If so, I imagine it the will of Nature. I realize I need to acquiesce to these laws and stop trying to control events that I have no control over; simply accept them with grace.

Turning to the river the magic of my inexplicable recovery is shattered like the skin of thin ice that is beginning to form at its fringes. I see my canoe being drawn off into the current. I am dumbstruck and stand arms extended, waiting for the correction in what I've seen to explain this. The free fall of horror scrapes away the scaffolding of anticipation I've built around tomorrow as I watch the canoe disappear around the bend.

My helpless confusion quickly transforms into a gut-wrenching realization: I am not getting out of here! It is too far and winter is here. My mind struggles for interpretation; order; reason. Shit, shit, shit! As fate slams the door, the darkness always accompanying resignation is lighted by the faint glow of recognition for my old friend irony. The river that has given me back hope, has heeled me and offered me a stake in the future, has now taken it all back.

I throw out a laugh which promotes me in the direction of the only true recovery: acknowledgement of my fate. Programmed denial and defense dissipate like cheap anger and I am granted the calm to sit here at the verge of my mortality.

Snow has begun to accumulate. The white surrounds me, I have stopped shivering, and I cast no shadow. Is shadow just the absence of light? I ask myself, devoid of matter and inconsequential. Qvus Washington would be proud of me here roosting in this moment. He was fond of reminding me, in his unbookish lingo, when I was dreading a pending firefight in the swamps of Nam, "When you're ruffled about what comes next, Private Shitbox, you're kissing goodbye to right now."

A lonely leaf gives up its grip on the mother tree and dances with the snowflakes and settles delicately in the current; a lottery winner, landing in the river for a once-in-a lifetime trip to the ocean. Like me it is only a bit of used up biotics returning to the Earth. Jesus, doesn't misery love company.

I lie back and cry out against the snowflakes, falling heavier now, an elegant stanza of Emily Dickenson. They bring a gentle clarity to my mind; euphony to my ears as my vision is blurred by snow gathering on my eye lashes:

'Because I could not stop for Death, he kindly stopped for me, the carriage held but just ourselves and immortality.'

.308

On the Wind River

Yukon Territories, Canada

Vince McDougall fully intended to kill that French son of a bitch who slept with his wife and stole his dog. He'd been on a delivery to Tok, Alaska, for the wild game processing house he drove for and got held up a couple of days by an earlier than usual snow in the mountains. When he returned to Dawson City, Charlotte was gone and so was Sadie, his prized Malamute. It only took a few questions to his neighbors to comprehend that Jacque Letrabre had spent the night.

Maxine, the barista at Mid-Night Sun Coffee, knew the worst part of everything that went on inside and outside the bedrooms of Dawson City. She eyed Vince with a whispered 'Oh No' as he bundled in that morning looking like he had just shit his pants or was about to.

"I know, Vince honey; don't pull your sword on me. I told you you'd need a surveillance camera trained on your bedroom door when you married Charlotte."

"Where is that slut?"

"She's gone like a looney at the store, honey, and now you're gonna ask me where's Jacque, right? Well, I hear the porcupine herd is on the move and he went out to bag a caribou, then he's taking his dog team through Mayo on his way up to the Wernecke Mountains."

"He's heading up to the Wind River to overwinter at his cabin, ain't he?"

"What he does every winter, honey—work that trap line of his."

"Where's that cabin, Maxine?"

"I never been, but I hear it's at the mouth of Bear River where it enters the Wind. You wanna square up with Jacque, honey, you best wait till after ice breakup next spring; let yourself cool off and decide if that woman is worth what you got in mind."

"It ain't Charlotte, Maxine, that French bastard stole Sadie. There ain't no next spring I'm waitin' on to settle that score!"

"There are other women, honey, and other dogs and I'd rather like to see you unfrozen and without no holes in ya, but your eyes tell me there ain't no holdin' you back."

Vince had moved north from Edmonton a few years before and was getting 'winterized' as he thought of it. He had come to the Yukon for a new start. He had brought his anxiety and low self confidence with him, but he had bagged his moose for two years in a row and had canoed some strong rivers. But this notion of riding horseback into McKlusky Lake and canoeing down the Wind River this late in the season would require good skills and better luck. His gamble for revenge at the expense of reason would be like staying in a high stakes game with a low-ball hand.

It would cost him his job—disappearing without permission—but he'd lost plenty of jobs before and had given up on the social graces that made others successful. Buying the horse from the Indians in Mayo would cost him his last dollars, but the cost to his health was uncertain. Uncertainty is an inescapable corollary of life, Charlotte had read to him out of one of her books.

Looking up from the village of Mayo he saw the termination dust on the Wernecke Mountains: winter was moving down those mountains to meet him. He packed what he could get on that horse: moose jerky, flour, rice, rubber rain gear, what wool he had and his .308 Browning rifle and rode for five days up into those mountains. He was in a foot of snow by the third day and he knew the ice would be forming on the lake and the river. The wild card was whether the old miner's canoe would still be there. It was customary, he heard, that the canoe had been left at McKlusky Lake for fishermen to use for the last 20 years.

As he hurriedly transferred his goods to the canoe that would have to be lined two miles down a rocky bastard of a creek to the river he thought, "There are two ways to acquire wisdom, the easy way, with a teacher, and painful way, by life experience."

"I'm far more inclined to learn than to be taught," he said out loud to himself. His history of troubles with women and employers had left him defensive and susceptible to panic attacks. He was having a doozie right now as he realized he was committing himself to that icy river. He slapped the horse on the ass, like he saw in old western movies, hoping it had the sense to return to Mayo, but more than likely it would get snared by a grizzly on the way down.

By the time he got to the river he'd bloodied his toes dragging that canoe over the cobble in that creek and wrenched both knees. Contentment pleases the body, but pain strengthens the mind, and his resolve was locked in.

The wind was blowing with purpose when he got to the river, directly up stream, out of the north, bringing the cold with it. "I understand why they call this bugger the wind," he mutters to himself.

The majesty of the valley he'd arrived at with its outrageous peaks and forested slopes moderated his sore knees and acerbic attitude and he was swept away from his angry and anxious self, like the current of that aquamarine river hurtling him downstream. He looked long into the two foot of fast blue water to the imbricated cobble of eroded stones of red, green, yellow, as the river washed over them like a misty watercolor print. For the moment he was present outside himself, free of the searing rage and gutted house of self-confidence that had driven him here and he reflected on something Charlotte told him Friedrich Nietzsche said; "Not everything that makes us feel good is good for us and not everything that hurts may be bad."

For several days Vince paddled against that witch of a wind off the Beaufort Sea, accompanied by sleet and snow stinging his face. The water was low; summer snowmelt hadn't yet given way to winter moisture and the river braided and adventured across that wide floodplain. He was forced to drag his canoe over numerous rocky shoals and out of dead channels. The ice that seethed down this river each spring had ripped trees out of its banks depositing them in dangerous logjams and sweepers that could spell disaster if you weren't alert and got caught in an inescapable current pulling you into one.

He was a few weeks late for the festival of color that adorned the quick fall of arctic autumn. The river willow were, except for a few clinging yellow leaves, bare and gray; the color of the boulders; the color of the sky.

The moose were all down near the river foraging on the last easy grub, and darkness, that heavy blanket of winter, was being pulled with skeptical quickness over every day. It had been advancing toward the totality of night at the alarming rate of 15 minutes a day since the equinox in June.

Mid-afternoon on his third day, only an hour before nightfall, he watched a pack of wolves drag down a yearling moose, marveled at their separation strategy, creating confusion to stage their attack; a study in energy conservation. The mother, once recovered from the melee, charged back hooves flailing to protect her child, the total for what she had to show from Nature's assignment, but it was too late. The wolves fled, will never stand in for the challenge of an angry moose and risk the injury that would become their demise. When the mother eventually leaves her calf the pack will return to feast.

The caribou had begun their return to the winter feeding grounds. It always amazed Vince that they could make a living in this frozen, god-forsaken place; that they could smell the reindeer lichen under the snow and root it out. Huge numbers of them came; the Bonnet Plum Herd had 5,000, the Porcupine Herd up to 200,000. But with broad cloven hooves that served as snowshoes and each hair a packet of insulaton, they were perfectly adapted. It was the four months of summer that was their biggest problem; the blood-sucking hordes of mosquitoes that they migrated south to escape.

The Gwitch'In Indians of this deep arctic north preferred caribou meat to moose; more filling, not so rich. Vince selected a yearling traversing a slope, 150 yards out, amongst a dozen adults and brought it down with a sweet shot from his .308. He loved that gun and was confident in his skills, easily bagging a moose or dal sheep each year.

Vince savored his reindeer steak after days of eating lifeless biscuits of unsalted bannock mixed with the last cloud berries and alpine blueberries of the season he foraged. As he built his fire in the snow he thought about the Jack London short story—his favorite—'To Build a Fire' in which a desperate prospector with frozen fingers was unable to keep his fire burning.

He slept rolled in a tarp he laid on a bed of river rocks he'd spread over what warmth was left from his fire. This all fed his anger, as it metastasized, leaving scar tissue of retaliation that would not allow forgiveness in any measure to surface up to his consciousness. He made the specter of Jacque Latrobe and his due suffering the bargain of his continuance.

The fourth day was colder still, would for only an hour or two exceed freezing temperatures. The fringe of ice along the river's edge grew and and continued to constrict the river as he floated north and east towards Fort McPherson, 450 Km away. He had not experienced winter this far north and although he could comprehend how critical every decision was to staying alive, the cold had eliminated the mosquitoes and what a joy it was not be hounded by the never ending haze of blood-letting vermin.

This cold and darkness bred an alternative plan, that he might, once he'd dispatched Letrabre, overwinter in his cabin; hunting and trapping, burning the wood he had put up for the winter. The consequences of next spring he imagined not a great difficulty; Letrabre would be gone, witnesses nonexistent. His story would be the story. It was a natural hazard of this lifestyle to break a leg working a trap line and to freeze to death.

The grizzly, shaggy in their winter coats, had come to the river the lowest point in the valley, to dig out the ground squirrel tunnels, seeking every available calorie for the coming winter hibernation. They paid little attention to him as he slid silently past on the quick current.

He hung as close as the encroaching ice would allow him to the right bank certain he had to be approaching Bear River. The leg of the caribou he'd shot had frozen and was useless to him now, but he dared not fire his gun for concern of alerting Letrabre, although it would have been easy to bag a ptarmigan, poorly camouflaged now in the awkward blotchy transition to winter white. The arctic hare without their completed winter coat, were plentiful as well and readily seen in contrast to the snow. The Gwitch'in, who had long resided in these mountains call the staple hare, 'little man who feeds everybody'.

That night he ate his bland bannock and shivered in his tarp burrito thinking hateful thoughts about Letrabre, himself and Charlotte. Yet he knew when he brought her to Dawson City from Edmonton that her discontentment would be an inevitable result. She missed too much; her bookish friends and their intellectual conversations. He tried to engage her, actually enjoyed hearing what she was reading, but he was in the end just a hick who thought Schopenhauer was a power tool manufacturer. He wasn't all that surprised that she fucked Letrabre; there had been no sex in their relationship for months, a relationship which had been boiled down to bickering: "Must we burn wood?", "Why can't we drive to Whitehorse on the weekends for dinner?", "Take those boots off when you come inside my house!"

To hell with her and good riddance, he thought. What good fortune brings us is all a loan anyway, subject to being recalled at anytime. But that French son of a bitch, Letrabre, he heard himself proclaim out loud, stealing my dog; that's surpassing my threshold and there is going to be hell to pay.

Ike, an Indian elder friend of his father's, told him survival could be as basic as having a fire ready to light when he awoke nearly frozen after a night in the North Country and he was glad he'd heeded that advice. It was all his stiff fingers could do to light his prepared fire the next morning. This was the day he was sure he'd come to Bear River. He remembered something Charlotte read to him by somebody named Seneca: 'Your mind should be sent out in advance to meet all possibilities. Expect anything, be prepared for everything.'

He knew Letrabre was a wary man who had many enemies; was a seasoned Yukoner, capable of taking care of himself. He would have to be cautious, have a plan and not at anytime be too self confident. It might be easier to plug Letrabre from a distance like he did that caribou calf, but the satisfaction he sought would come from watching Letrabre grovel; beg for his life.

He held tight to the ice on the right bank so as not to be seen before he saw. He was nearly upon Bear River when he saw the smoke from Letrabre's fire hanging leisurely and low in the spruce trees, like a fart on a still day. The smoke illustrated the incongruence of this boreal forest, what the natives called the 'Drunk Forest'. The active layer, that two foot or less of thawed soil above the permafrost, provided tentative purchase for the scrubby black spruce, so they grew not vertical, as we expect trees to, but leaning off in all sorts of angles from horizontal.

Vince beached his canoe when he first saw the smoke and with rifle in tow climbed up off the river where he could learn his lay. The Bear River was a small, fast-flowing mountain stream that poured itself, name and all, into the Wind. He had a clear view of the cabin just across that river. It was a squat structure of logs with a mossy roof that reached nearly to the ground. There were a few spar windows and a porch. The rusted chimney came out of the roof at an angle to match the drunken forest and spewed white smoke. "Open the draft, dumbshit," Vince muttered to himself. Behind the cabin rose a tower on four tree spars with sheetmetal wraps; the food cache that bears couldn't access.

A lean-to of new, but poor, construction sat back in the trees near the latrine. It was full to the top with seasoned fire wood. Vince estimated over four cord of wood—enough for a comfy winter.

Chained to the surrounding trees was Letrabre's sled team. As was common, the dogs had little or no shelter, were hopelessly limited in movement as their chains were wound about the trees they were tied to. They were all separated to prevent fights. Vince saw Sadie, wet in the snow, but lunging, as were all the others, on their short leashes, howling and yelping, setting up a hellacious ruckus. They had apparently seen him or heard him. He crouched lower in the brush and watched as Letrabre came out to investigate.

With his rifle at the ready Letrabre stood on the porch in clear view, maybe 200 yards away; a clean shot. He wore a plaid shirt and his customary green beret, his pipe clenched in his teeth. He scanned the bluff across the Bear River where Vince squatted motionless. Letrabre then retreated back into his cabin.

Vince returned to where his canoe was beached, bushwhacked his way to the mouth of the Bear and forded it as best he was able. It was cold and swift and he was swept off his feet several times. It disturbed him that his .308 went swimming with him. He was uncertain if this dousing would affect its functioning. Once he was across, his uncontrollable shivering alerted him that he was in the early stages of hypothermia. It would be imperative that he find himself by a fire soon or he would lose the edge of reason, when his desires might fall outside reality.

Staying clear from view of any of the cabin windows he slunk,(if you prefer slinked, fine), his way off the river and around to the cabin, out of sight of the dogs. As he was about to step onto the porch he reached down and picked up a rock. The dogs had settled down as their view of him was blocked by the cabin.

Vince felt his heart racing; he sought control of his breathing. He held his .308 in his right hand and the rock in the other. Exterior doors typically open in, for the sake of space, however, this door opened onto the porch. Vince, rife with anxiety, stood so he would be hidden by the door when it opened and threw the rock so it banged and rattled off the stoop. The door opened slowly, the barrel of Letrabre's rifle was first to emerge. Vince waited until Letrabre stepped beyond the door and stabbed the .308 into his ribs.

"Drop it like an ugly woman you shitdammit."

Letrabre let the rifle fall to the porch and Vince stepped away. "Let's go into the warm and have a chat."

"Chat," Letrabre's Quebecois accent sweetened even the bitterness of his expression, "You pees of sheet, I know thees chat already."

Vince sat within the immediate radiation of the stove, resting his .308 across the arm of the chair aimed directly at Letrabre sitting against the opposite wall.

"You stole my dog, you Francaphonie pretender, and you fucked my wife. Did you really think you were going to cozy away your winter without answering the call?" Vince felt his ire, that subtle furnace for burning off anger, rising.

"You pees of sheet, are the pretender. You ruin thees dog; it leeves in your house. Thees dogs are sled dogs. Thees dogs leeve in the snow! And you woman, you pees of sheet, only she look at mee pants and she drops hers." Letrabre waved his head as though adamantly denying as he released his affected laugh. His lime eyes were squeezed closed, his shaggy gray beard swam with the gesture.

"Beg for mercy asshole or I'll put a slug in the pocket of your cute little Yukon shirt."

Letrabre spit on the floor. "To be afraid to die ees to be dead already. See what you are? You drive a leedle truck, you pees of sheet, you wear a leedle safety strap and buy your deener in a store. I keel what I eat, I sleep when I'm tired, nobody geeves me a day off. The present has no eend—who else can you say thees about?"

"Listen, Letrabre, you're talkin' pretty loud for havin' a .308 aimed at your heart. Maybe you wanna tone it down a bit, Aye?"

"Shoot me, you pees of sheet! But first let me geeve you advice. If you tie a dog to a cart hees going to follow it, hees got no choice. Eef you tie me to that cart, I climb on it and take control. You see Veence I got thees sheet in my heart, but if we tie you to that cart you fight the rope, try to go another direction and eend up strangling your dumb ass. You only theenk you are in control. Be the dog Veence. Follow the cart. Queet trying to be me."

"What the fuck does that mean, Letrabre?" This was just the thing to knock Vince off any run of confidence he might have been having.

"Eeet means, Veence, go back to town, find a woman dumber than you. There must be one, maybe two. Drive your leedle truck and don't try to be me." Letrabre was doing that reverse nodding of the head that says real clearly that there is a challenge on the table.

"Geeve me that rope. I weel tie one hand to thees chair. Then you can come over heere and tie the other hand. Then steeal my food, and my rifle, anything you want. Sleenk to your canoe, you coward. In seven days, eef you are not afraid or lazy, you can paddle to the eend of the Weend to the

Peel River and then seven more days to Fort Mcpheerson and home and
your pleasure."

Jacque began tying his left wrist to the chair, smiling of course. Vince
felt the emptiness of his insecurity, and like his shadow it followed him,
expanding and diminishing with light and darkness. He cherished the
warmth generated when he felt in control, but could never relax in it because
a word, even the slightest hesitancy, would tumble him into this reality of
inadequacy. With the recent events, with Charlotte, Sadie, Jacque, he felt a
great pain of depreciation, felt it pushing him—like the taunts of a peer—to
fight back.

"It's not pleasure I seek, Jacque, it's just the absence of pain…and you are
my pain."

The fire of his anger burned through him again and he clenched his teeth to
it; with the clench came the squeeze. The report of the rifle startled him and
it fell to the floor. He opened his mouth to the breath that rushed into him.
He blinked to focus on Jacque, slumped over himself, blood wicking into his
plaid shirt.

It was done. The consequences were out of his control. He felt the release of
tension, like drilling through the nail of a distended finger; sensed the
comfort in that, felt it mix with a dread of how things might end. It stole into
him, like caffeine in a silent coup takes control of your attention.

But for now the dogs were his responsibility. He felt thankful for that task,
a physical handle to grab onto like the handle of a door swinging closed.
He knew their diet must vary; constant moose meat is too rich. It would be
necessary to shoot caribou and of course he would feed them Jacque.

EXILE:
MOSKITO COAST, NICARAGUA

Every Garden Has Its Snakes

Written in:

San Juan del Norte, Nicaragua

His wife is a goner. The dementia is full-blown and she doesn't know him from the janitor. The full-care facility comes in at $4K per month and his daughter, always a mama's girl, sees after her. His role is financial; he sold the house they had lived in for 40 years and surrendered it all to his daughter. Still more is needed. His $600 a month social security check is not enough for him to live on and still help with the mounting expenses of his wife's care, so he searched for a cheaper place to live and it led him to San Juan del Norte at the mouth of the San Juan River in Nicaragua.

He speaks but rudimentary Spanish so he doesn't communicate with anyone outside of a few sputtering words to La Doña Jimenez, his landlady. He rents a tiny room in her stilted house which was once blue, but is now worn and moldy bare wood. La Doña cooks his simple meals of rice and beans, fish—if he catches any—and fried breadfruit, for which he has developed an affinity. There is one egg for breakfast and again rice and beans, called Gallo Pinto here and eaten every day by every person.

His total room and board each month is $150. Each afternoon he drinks precisely 200 ml of Flor de Caña, good Nicaraguan rum. This costs him an additional $120 a month, which he has absolutely no problem rationalizing given that goods are expensive here as all cargo must be brought in by water. He must take the slow boat 12 hours upriver to San Carlos once each month to withdraw his social security money out of an ATM. This costs him $25. While he is there he transfers $200 to his daughter. The remaining $100 he keeps hidden in his room, letting it accumulate for his retirement. He has a good laugh at this gesture and remembers that he once thought of life as a stagecoach to be held up and as much loot as possible taken from it in preparation for the future. He enjoys the illusion he worked from that there was something to be gained from the future that wasn't available in the present. Time was once a cherished commodity to him; he now thinks of time as the snake in his Eden that must be endured and devotes his life to killing it.

Because it is too expensive, he has stopped taking the medicine for his heart; a heart he imagines will drop him dead one day. 'Better than dying with a hose in my nose,' he hears himself rationalize. Indeed his very tranquil existence away from electricity, cars, noise and especially his daughter have improved his health. His daughter began to displace him at her birth; an Aphrodite goddess he always thought, with a servant: him, carrying a mirror before her so she could constantly see herself. She introduced darkness into his patriarchy. She had avoided the domination of all outer men; was therefore dominated by the inner man, the animus that C.G. Jung suggested lived in every woman. This masculine shadow was cast deep into her landscape leaving her self-centered and willful. Along with the absence of his daughter's influence, he credits the alcohol with his well-being, but whatever it is, he has been discharged from the battle we all wage unsuccessfully against natural entropy. He has gone over to the enemy; makes no attempt to think good thoughts about his self-indulgent daughter or his braindead wife; does not consider physical consequences when making personal decisions and has eliminated all efforts to live without fear or greed for which he labored much of his life for fearful or greedy reasons.

When he arrived here he bought a battered dugout ponga that he named Carmencita after the first woman he had sex with, and the only woman who ever showed any appreciation for this kindness. He putts out across the wide Rio Indios each morning to fish, then hikes the sendero through the jungle a few hundred meters to the Caribbean coast. Here he walks along the deserted beach and watches the ships passing close to shore en route to and from Limon, Costa Rica and Bluefields, Nicaragua.

He wears the same threadbare shorts every day. His sagging skin is baked black by the tropical sun during the dry season from January through May and soaked by the ubiquitous rain during the wet season. It rains over 15 feet a year here in the jungle, not worth mentioning he realizes, when considering Cherrapunji, India, which sees 40 feet a year. With the constant sun and water he imagines he is rotting away at about the same rate as his soon-to sink ponga.

These future considerations concern him not. The present is the only thing that has no end.

And so he thinks nothing of his certainly impending death; knows it is upon him. As with the heart medicine, he cannot afford the anti-seizure medicine. The seizures come more frequently and he understands that if one pours over him while he is in his little ponga he may fall out and be claimed by the river; if not the little motor will take him where it wishes. Usually he awakens from a seizure disremembering, tongue bit and bleeding, somewhere on the beach or in town, children watching wide-eyed from a distance.

He can tolerate death, but not laziness, which he considers the ultimate form of fear. And so every morning he drags his aching body across the river and through the jungle to walk for hours along the coast. He keeps as high as he can on the beach, especially if the tide is coming in, to remain out of reach should he seize.

On Christmas Day, warm with partial sun after a heavy rain, he sees a white littering in the surf ahead, knows it can't be foam but must be cargo from a ship in trouble. Only after coming upon the scene of dancing white plastic and breaking one open, letting the kilogram of fine white powder chafe out and disperse across the surf, does he comprehend what he has come upon.

He is aware that the Moskito Coast, along this rugged and little peopled section of the Caribbean, is a principal transfer point for the cocaine trade, so it isn't a far leap to visualize a small craft capsizing or even narcotrafficers dumping the cargo if the heat were on. It is even an easier reach to expect them to come looking for millions of dollars of cocaine.

For this reason he spends the next three days gathering all 81 packages, leaving no trace, as he wraps each in banana leaves and hides them in the dense jungle just up from the beach and carrying four at a time in burlap sacks (he knows them as gunny sacks, Nicaraguans call them coffee sacks) across the narrow peninsula to his ponga.

He changes his daily routine after this—walks a different stretch of the coast, keeps himself out of the attention of the searchers. But, he knows them when they come to San Juan Nicaragua. They are not the tourists who come to fish for tarpon, or government officials to administer to La Reserva Indo-Maize, thousands of acres of natural rain forest that surround this remote place.

These interlopers are well dressed men asking questions. Desperation is in their eyes. When one approaches him where he docks his ponga, he understands none of the rapid-fire Spanish and responds with his usual shrug and poorly accented, "No entiendo."

Doña Marquez later explains during one of their rudimentary conversations of Spanglish and mime, that they were who he suspected. These drug traffickers provide him with an enemy he realizes we all need to define ourselves. He takes her to her dead husband's carpentry shop and shows her the 81 kilos of cocaine he has secreted away. She sits in shock on one of the million dollar bundles, hand on her forehead, mouth agape.

He understands her question because she repeats it over and over, "¿Que hacerlo, señor, que hacerlo?"

"Voy a darte." He thinks he has said he is giving it to her.

"Necesito nada, señor. Soy una viejita, pero la gente de la puebla estan muy pobre."

He understands several words: *'viejita'*: she is old and needs nothing, and *'la gente pobre'*: poor people of the village. So he forms a context, smiles his recognition. He admires in her the miraculous force love plays, wanting nothing for herself, thinking only of the people of her village and decides he will donate all but one million to them. He does not compute the difficulty of converting 180 pounds of someone else's cocaine into Nicaraguan cordobas, for that is the future and he is firmly planted in the present.

He then sprinkles a pinch of his new treasure on the back of his hand and huffs it into his nose. His smile expands as he imagines the reaction of his daughter, who has always thought of him as a weak man, a loser, when he hands her $1 million.

"If not for we losers there would be no winners," he whispers.

Mormons

Written in:

Orinoco, Nicaragua

Dear Sis,

It is January 1999 when I write this. I know you've not heard from me for a long, long time, and I apologize for that. I write now that I sense death has crept into my house.

They are here for me now and the end is upon me. Some voice in me is insisting that someone knows where I am and what happened to me. Patsy's death was officially determined to be accidental, but they know I killed her and now they've come for me.

Old Danny the dimwit handyman isn't all that dim. People think that because he can't talk, he can't hear and understand something. He had no trouble understanding that I wanted him to loosen the connection on the propane line in our basement. Propane, unlike natural gas, is heavier than air and it filled up our basement like a swimming pool. When she came back to Newland and turned up her thermostat, it sparked the furnace pilot light and the house blasted off like a rocket ship. The explosion was so massive two neighboring houses burned. These things happen to old houses.

The abandonment, her rebuke, the dark hole left in me was far more than I was prepared to bear. You know she not only ran away to Bountiful, B.C. with that fundamental Mormon polygamous guy, Dolan, she also moved in with his other wives and she married him while we were still married.

Dolan had a revelation from God, he said, that she should become his wife. 'He is a criminal,' I pleaded, 'polygamy is against the law!'

God's law trumps man's law, she said.

His prophet, Joseph Smith, 100 years ago, told him that a man who doesn't have at least three wives (celestial wives he called them) will not be granted entrance into heaven. What a crock of shit. Joseph Smith, Brigham Young and all the rest were just exploitative lechers.

Well, God spoke to me too. "Kill that bitch!" He said, "You're not getting into my heaven until her blood runs."

Well, where I am now is hell and the only god I can know is me.

So I knew they'd come for me. FLDS are a vengeful cult. Look at the Fancher wagon train in 1857: Dressed up like Paiute Indians they massacred women and children. And now, the Lafferty brothers in Utah cut the throat of a baby and her mother in 1984 because their god told them to.

So I have hidden myself here on the Miskito Coast of Nicaragua among the black Garifuna people of Orinoco and Bluefields. You come here by boat or plane; there are no roads into this jungle. I have pasted together a paranoid existence here. There is no need for Spanish language; a rich English Creole is spoken. I don't understand it, but they all understand me and they are able to relax the dialect sufficiently so I understand their English. I am seldom communicated with. Isn't this the perfect definition of psychosis: insufficiently shared reality to comprehend the facts of my own reality. These people survive their difficult existence with a shared humor. My schizophrenic oddity lives outside all of this.

I have one acquaintance of these people, a man named Chamy, who is an outcast by virtue of some crime he hasn't shared with me. I drink the rum with him, but we share little else; my desire not to get drunk alone maybe the remaining residue of my sanity.

Chamy knows why I am here; I am hiding from the Mormons. I explained what they'll look like: two young men in white shirts and neckties. He had no idea what a necktie was, so I described it to him. He then asked, "What are they for and why are they worn?"

It is difficult to explain a necktie to a man, like most Garifuna men, who wear an old pair of flip flops, or goes barefoot and has no shirt. I tell him neckties are objects of unearned authority and serve no physical function. They are like a necklace, only adornments. Neckties, I told him, are worn by people who want you to feel beneath them. It gives them power. I hope I got this right.

On one of his weekly trips into Bluefields—a bigger town but still very remote and backwards—Chamy saw the Mormons. He said everybody was talking about them and laughing (Garifuna laugh at everything). These white boys were like two painted boards on an old fence, he told me, walking together through the dirty streets carrying bibles. He said he's impressed that they have many wives, while he can get no woman. He asked if I can get him a necktie.

It is difficult for him to imagine that they are here to kill me because they look like clowns. But I know it won't be long before they find me, so I have begun this letter to you. I will write more if I have time. Chamy will mail it when I am gone.

Orinoco is a jungle town of 1200 people and no cars. It is tucked deep in the Pearl Lagoon of the Atlantic Coast. Dirt pathways meander past broken wooden houses on stilts with no glass in the windows. Tethered horses and goats keep the open spaces open where happy, nearly naked children play soccer and fly kites. A long, deteriorating dock stretches out into the bay. Little girls with corn rows and homemade dresses dance hopscotch and play with plastic sack dolls. Young boys fish for dinner off the dock. Fish, shrimp or lobster are eaten at every meal. Nobody can afford other meat. All fruit, like bananas and malacuya, is collected from the jungle. Along with the birds, laughter can always be heard.

I live in the tallest building in Orinoco, on the second floor of a tattered boarding house near the dock. I am the only white man. I have seen no other white men here. The townspeople leave me alone, as in excluded, but they are not mean to me.

From my window I have the spectacular view of the jungle-fringed Pearl Lagoon. I also have a clear view of the dock so I see everybody who comes and goes on the twice-weekly boat to Bluefields.

There is no way I can hide here, a marshmallow in a bowl of black beans, but I have the advantage of knowing when they arrive in town. Chamy and I have devised a trap.

Chamy has watched the Mormons in Bluefields, has told me they go business to business, door to door pitching their god. Or, Chamy suggests, maybe they're asking about any white men who live here.

It doesn't matter because they will eventually find me—come to my door—the first door they'll come to in Orinoco when getting off the boat. When they come to my door they will kill me or I will kill them.

Always, your brother

Dear Sis,

It is now February and I have sat at my window for nearly a month watching the dock; watching for the Mormons. I was beginning to think they weren't looking for me after all, only proselytizing, but they came.

When they got off the boat, the people of Orinoco stepped back and stared. These two young men, with their pink skin, white shirts and neckties, were so conspicuously different in contrast to the black faces that a siren might as well have sounded.

They walked right past my building at the end of the dock and disappeared down the muddy path into the village. Chamy and I prepared our trap to be ready when they came back. I don't know where they intended to stay because the boat would not return for two days. Maybe they thought they would stay in my room at the boarding house after they killed me.

I was vigilant all that afternoon, because I knew they were coming. Chamy started yakking like he does when he wants some of my rum. I'm watching out the window for the Mormons and he's chattering away.

"Like my papa, mon, he so old he shit his self, caint do nofin fer his self, mama gotta do fer him like a baby — so there you is, he so wore out, mon, he come round to near the same spot he was brand new."

"What's the point of your story, Chamy, or are you just talking?"

"Maybe yo happy place right next to yo pain, mon?"

"This is bullshit, Chamy. Look at your miserable-assed life; you don't even got shoes. You got no family, no money, you eat off of me, drink my rum, you don't even like me. Why are you always laughing and happy? It is just a big show isn't it?"

"Just hit me wit a rock, mon. dat hurt. Yo breakin' my neurons, mon. I got da choosin' to be pleasured or pained, why I wanta be pained?"

"Look out the window down there at those leaf cutter ants, Chamy, right there a whole highway of them, each carrying a chewed off leaf to their queen. Then they'll go back for more,for miles to get the right leaves. Chances are they'll get stepped on or licked up by an anteater, or die of exhaustion…just like us— ants in a meaningless existence doing meaningless shit for what? For nothing; it is all for somebody else, the man, the government, but it doesn't seem we get much for our efforts."

"I dunt knows most, like yo knows, but I knows da best a all yo knows."

"What's the best, Chamy?"

"Yo right, boss, dem ants don't know happy…what yo says you be look for, happy, that aint notin cept preacher talk. Dem ants way up on we, ya see, mon, we gotta get free of dat spectin' to be happy, like dem ants start off wit no happy talk from der mamas, we gotta figger happy ain't part of da deal, mon, like shittin' and fuckin', and soons yo figger it, yos free, mon. Nuttin lef but enjoy da moon shinin cross da bay, mon, a perdy woman strollin pass ya, laughin in ya belly when ya sees somesbody hit on da head wit a coconut…best is just a chair and sum a dat golden rum. Yo gots some a dat golden rum, mon?"

"Well, I envy you Chamy, living life so simple as not to be looking forward to anything, just ready to enjoy what might come upon you. But these fundamentalist Mormons, they settle their scores. You ever see these missionary boys here before?"

"Whats sa misinsary mean, mon?"

"Missionary is what those Mormon boys in their neckties are. Out beating their drums trying to flush out every last heathen in the bushes so they can tell them they've got it all wrong—that what they believe is bad. That the real God is the Mormon God, and they try to convert them. It is the same as someone coming here and convincing you that you can walk on water then getting you to walk into the ocean. That's what they are—missionaries—and you should be on your watch out!"

"Never seed em 'fore."

"That's right, they are here looking for me, to kill me."

"I got couples a thinkin' on dat. Firs, mon, yo gotta get good wit dyin. Aint til den yo can enjoy. Yo ain't no mor look 'head den at yor feet, spectin' sompin good gonna happen. Just take da banana outta yor hand right now.

I dunt know, mon, yo be hook up real good to da back a da wagan. Da wagan draggin yo down da street, yo fightin agin' it. Just a well follow da wagan n be easy as fight agin it."

"What you can't change you must endure, is that what you're saying?"

"Don't know dem words, mon. Soun like preacher word ta me."

"You said you had two thoughts on what I said, Chamy. What's the other one?"

"Well, boss, yos perdy hard on dem Mornman fellas. What I believin' in? I believin' yo got rum in yo cupboard. What yo believe? Yo believe folk is affer ya, an yo hidin' like a rabbet. Maybe I wanna talk wit dem boys; maybe I kan git me one of dem neckties. You hide up der wit yo hand on da snake rope, so yo ain't so skerd. I come back drink da splash a rum."

So Chamy went off to talk with the Mormons. I stayed right here looking out my upstairs window, watching for them and going over our plan.

There is only one other tenant in the boarding house, Lazy Joe, the school teacher, but there was no school now because it was the long winter break, and he was gone.

The plan is for Chamy to answer their knock, but now he may actually bring them back with him, so I have to be ready when they come. He will maneuver them to the base of the stairs. When they are standing at just the right spot I will spring the trap, releasing the net holding the seven Terciopelo that Chamy has captured.

Bothrops asper, Central America's Lancehead, with their yellow tipped tails and aggressive temperaments, are the ultimate pit vipers. They are drawn into the village by the rats. Several children have been bitten by them and died since I've been here. The closest anti-venom is in Bluefields three hours away, too far to get to in time. Members of the Fer de Lance family, they hold enough venom for multiple bites and their long fangs inject it deep into a man's tissue. The anti coagulant in the venom causes immediate internal hemorrhaging and constriction of the throat.

So our Mormon hitmen will be soon writhing and screaming on the floor, their bibles full of Joseph Smith's revelations lying uselessly next to them.

In the darkness of early morning when the village is sleeping, Chamy and I will carry the bodies along the bay to the village dump where the Terciopelo hunt for rodents. The children are warned never to play near here, but these two Mormon white men obviously didn't know this and the people of the village will see they were killed by the snakes.

Hours went past before I saw Chamy coming out of the village and onto the dock. No Mormons, just Chamy coming along with that cockeyed, prancing gait of his, like there's music playing somewhere. I studied him like I hadn't before, and I was thinking I do like him. He's the blackest man I've ever seen; barefoot and rib-skinny with that pile of dirty dreadlocks pouring out of his little head and down to his waist. It made we wonder how he keeps from just tipping over.

When he walked in he shouted upstairs to me, "I comin', don pull dat snake rope. Comin' sip on dat rum."

"Where are those Mormons? What are they scheming on?"

"They stayin' in da shed a Auntie Sanya. She ain't takin no money, 'spect she like da tention dem two boys is bring in. Sure is pink, ain't dey?"

"They know about me, don't they? When are they coming?"

"Dem boys ain't look fer ya; dem boys don no yos here. Dey sellin' som place call heven. Says woman all necket der in heven, n Chamy buyin' hiself a ticket. Maybes yos buy a ticket like me, wes sit ta gether in heven n drinks ya rum, watch dem necket womans. Mama she says ta us chillen, when slicegrass cut yo foots, pick som dat same slicegrass n rubs on da cut, make betta what it don hurt. Maybes, cause dem Morman boys don yo hurt, dey zackly what yo need rub on dat hurt."

Well, Sis, Chamy may be right.

Sincerely,

Your brother.

ROMANCE:
ARIZONA CENTRAL HIGHLANDS

The Mountains Are Calling Me

Written at:

Granite Mountain, Prescott, AZ

Imagine the cabin. 'Rustic' my husband called it, but it was falling down. Flies and mice and lizards shared it with me. All welcome. A piece of the wearing down of my life; aches of aging, loss of the beauty I was convinced I once held replaced by gray hair, glasses and a thickening around the middle. My husband's passion was lost to pain, adult children no longer needed me, and the insidious linger of a life wasted.

A partner in demise, the cabin demanded of me to sit down, watch the birds, leave maintenance and planning to its own company. The screened porch and a creaky old rocking chair, stacks of read and unread novels, cold coffee cups and the morning and afternoon sun, were perfect for day dreaming.

Three rooms; the great room—hardly great, a bathroom, where I had to hold my arms to my sides to slide into, and a bedroom dominated by an east and west facing windows that opened to the afternoon breeze lifting the fading sheer curtains in a gauze of interpretive dance. A faint fragrance of mothballs held the exotic history of 70 years of sleep, dreams and romance, that little room had witnessed.

Each morning I would lay the spread of yellow chenille—charming in translation to caterpillar in French—across the bed, smoothing its wrinkles. This provided what little order my newly transformed life required, allowing the worn floor to be unswept; the chipped porcelain sink to hold a days' worth of dirty dishes.

Early each afternoon I would walk along the creek excusing itself through the pine and cottonwood trees. I joined its ramble and burble over and around stones of red and yellow, eroded smooth by the repeating cycle of water. Molecules of a single purpose, to return to the mother ocean. Tanagers, nuthatches, and occasionally the stately statue of a green heron perching on one leg patiently watching for a silver feast to swim through the placid pool. My little red cabin, patient like the heron, waited my return.

Coming around the sweeping bend in the creek I would see the cabin perfectly framed by boughs, a Rembrandt light illuminating its humble persistence. It belonged there as sure as the sky.

Certainly there would be deer browsing in the clearing it occupied. A wisp of chimney smoke rose on cold winter days. A forest service cabin, calm, bucolic and intended, it was deeded to me by Miami Pittman, the dear old neighbor woman in Prescott, childless and alone, whom I cared for the last years of her life.

And now that my husband has returned to his law firm and is consumed in his personal battle with arthritis, I have retreated to the cabin and this new and appreciated relationship with myself.

Dutiful daughter of a demanding mother, I had lived her scripture-infused proper existence, looking good from the outside.

My father, a yielding man of uncompromised empathy, encouraged me to pursue what felt magic. So I read. I read everything: the backs of boxes, Tolkien, John D McDonald. I fell in with words and was fulfilled. But when I married I attached myself to the role my mother groomed me for, the good wife, sacrificing my interests and career for family and children.

On this clear, cool afternoon, returning from my creek wander I became aware, really for the first time, of the toll of autumn; the creek's flow was reduced; the cottonwood leaves hinting of gold. As I usually do, I stopped at the edge of the forest to look up across the green meadow to watch deer and their graceful high stepping through the grass.

I saw the man standing at the cabin door.

A rare visitor; anybody this far off the traveled network of convenience, percolated a suspicion in me. I watched from my safe window of nature. I will just wait until he leaves.

He didn't try the door; unlocked, as it always was. He didn't peer with cupped hand to the brow into the dirty window. He just stood there looking down on the green basin of the creek valley.

He was not dressed like a vagabond or a man without bearing. He looked from this distance like the photographs I'd seen of Walt Whitman; a large brimmed hat, full beard and longish gray hair. He wore a knapsack and held a walking stick.

My rebellious daughter was fond of quoting Whitman, from Leaves of Grass: "Resist much, obey little!" This was how I remembered it. 'Leaves of grass' had an indisputable affect on me as I transitioned from the deferential wife into a person.

It is amusing how we judge new interactions based on previous acquaintances with similar traits and appearances. I rejected a potential friendship not many months ago because a new member of my Master Gardener's group looked too much like my captious mother-in-law. In this circumstance the man's appearance who was standing at my door reminded me of photos I'd seen of Walt Whitman, who I had a good impression of, and I felt my anxiety ease.

I abandoned my decision to wait this uninvited guest out when he sat in the old rusted Lloyd's chair next to the cabin door. He crossed one long leg over the other, removed his hat and rocked as though intending to stay.

I approached the cabin through the trees in the back so as not to be seen crossing the open slope on the confirmed path up to where he sat. I held at the back corner of the cabin and listened. He was humming Gershwin's, 'Summertime', the song my father sang to his children when he cooked.

I was compelled out of the shadows by a curiosity I couldn't deny and a familiarity I couldn't identify. With an unaccustomed step into vulnerability not away from it, I walked around the cabin to stand in the sunny spot in front of where he sat and said, "Hello."

He stood, turned to me and bowed modestly. His eyes, the source of reference we so depend on in assessment, were blue; a penetrating blue like Paul Newman's eyes. Deep smile lines broadcast out from them. He had a gentle face, well tanned. I judged him to be in his early 60's.

He apologized in a soft voice, a bit of Australian accent, maybe New Zealand. He apologized again and held out the yet unexposed left hand. It was wrapped in a blood stained paisley handkerchief. He had snagged his hand on a New Mexican Locust bush, genus Robinia, whose lovely pink flowers belie its nasty thorns.

One of these thorns had laid the flesh back on his hand and he was having difficulty stopping the bleeding. He asked if I had alum, turmeric or even gauze.

There was nothing presumptuous about his manner or request other than his mention of turmeric as a styptic whichI had never heard of before.

With the new found perspective that was bundled in the package of release that came with my time at the cabin, the long inculcated wariness my mother and husband had instilled in me washed across my consciousness and dissipated like insincere clouds. I invited him in to sit at the tiny nook in the kitchen corner of the cabin.

I tended to his hand, cleaning the wound, wrapping it in gauze and applying pressure with my left hand. His fingers were long and delicate with clean, trimmed nails.

"You play the piano," I said.

It wasn't a question, rather an assumption of certainty. Smiling he studied my eyes for a moment saying only, "And you are a gardener."

"There's dirt under my nails?" I asked.

"No, certainly not. You have hands like my mother's; strong, that look of familiarity with tools."

With this we fell into a conversation: his long dead wife, my long ago grown children, his literature studies at what he named the Lyceum. I made tea and apologized for the sink full of dirty dishes, a habit of my mother's to apologize for less than absolute tidiness in her home.

"What's a sink but a vessel of accumulation?" He suggested.

I asked him why he was hiking here so far off the main trail. He said his motivation was to spend a night in the forest with only his wits. A student of John Muir's, he wanted to be in the world more not just on it.

I told him of a sheltered meadow next to the cliff downstream about a mile that would collect the first rays of morning sun. I asked if he had food and he laughed that he had nothing, but certainly we can endure twelve hours without eating, and be better for it. He would drink from the creek and build a shelter of brush and a bed of boughs.

He felt that along with age and an ever-more convenient life, he had begun to lose a connection with nature and needed to be reintroduced to that relationship. He expressed how lucky he thought I was to have found myself in such close company with the birds and the trees. He envied this. Wondered whether I had grandchildren and if they spent time with me here.

I explained I did have grandchildren, but they were uncomfortable here out of cell phone service and with no television. We mused on the loss of relationships with nature on younger generations; how important it was for imagination and wonder to be out of human influence. And so we tracked the lengthening rays of late August sun across the cabin floor. Talked of time and gossamer.

We considered the coyotes and their generalist adaptations of population to man's predation and famine. I related a dream of a peaceful world with only women leaders—a notion I had recently offered to apathetic audiences poorly chosen. But here in his congruent presence I felt an unspoken acceptance, a freedom of motion I hadn't experienced since childhood.

No silent reception this time. He smiled his agreement and commented only that we need to look no further than the matriarchal and successful social communities of wolves to see I was right.

He asked me about spending so much time alone here at the cabin. I explained I had become very selective in who I spend my time with, limiting that expenditure to those who had something to say that I could learn from. And with that decision I had selected my own company.

I asked how he had decided to seek first aid at the cabin. His wound was not an emergency. He had spotted the cabin from the trail far above, he said. Its old, unimproved windows and invitational screened porch had compelled him to approach. While he explained, I freed my eyes to explore the interior of the cabin, what familiarity had blinded me to. My eyes roamed past the deeply ambered pine of the walls and ceiling to the elegantly designed Guatemalan rugs of vibrant primary colors I had affixed here and there to those walls that surprised you with their bold voice like Pavarotti singing a hymn with the congregation.

I found the dead flies on the window sills and ash spilling out of the fireplace, evidence that something was happening here; there was life.

When he got up to use the bathroom I hurried into the bedroom to sweep my personal articles out of sight, smooth the chenille cover, knowing he would be looking directly into the bedroom when he came out of the bathroom. I moved quietly. I imagined him listening in the charged silence of new discovery.

When he emerged I was just coming out of the bedroom. He stepped near, looked past me at the curtains floating in the breeze. He wore an expression of remembering, as though of a melody recalled or of youth.

"Lovely," He uttered in a dreamy manner, "how these little curtains and an open window can satisfy me like all the words cannot."

I stepped back into the room, an invitation I hadn't consciously intended. He slipped politely past me to stand at the window taking in the verdant view of my morning awakenings.

I moved next to him. Our hands inadvertently touched and little fingers curled together as naturally as water moves over stone.

"When one tugs at a single thing in nature he finds it attached to the rest of the world." He spoke without looking at me, "An observation of John Muir's, but there are events the power of our imaginations make separate, endearingly isolated. We must look past how far we can see."

He embraced me. I welcomed his nearness. Laying my head back I let the breeze move my hair. His lips found an immediate home in the suprasternal notch at the base of my throat, like a saucer of warm milk a kitten hunches over to lap up with a pink tongue.

I fell open like a favorite book begging to be read, every syllable pronounced, understood and lingered over. Eagerness took us deeply. I remember fine strands of his hair stuck to my cheek; his saying that flesh is the most exquisite poetry. I was taken away, and upon my return, waking in the morning, I hadn't recalled being away.

I found only his note: 'The mountains are calling me. I must go. John Muir.'

Snaps

Written in:

Pocatello, Idaho

Let's not even debate whether it was heroic or not, it wasn't. Inconvenient it was, and frightening, but not heroic.

I saw the taillights well over a mile ahead as I crested the pass coming down into town that night of the 2012 presidential election. They weren't where I would have expected the highway to be and they weren't moving. Somebody had pulled off on a side road, had stopped to open a gate possibly, but it was difficult to imagine a road branching off the highway here on this steep descent into town.

I lost sight of the taillights as I rounded a corner, but slowed down to look for them where I imagined I saw them. There was a steep slope off the south side of the road here and I could see nothing but the blackness of the forest below. I crept ahead and soon came to the skid marks leading over the edge.

I pulled over onto the narrow shoulder, activated my emergency flashers, and walked around behind my car. The exhaust rising past the bright flashing emergency lights prevented a clear view of where the road ended and the abyss began. I rested my hand on the car and baby-stepped to the break.

The darkness below was illuminated only by the two glowing taillights several hundred feet below.

I swore for the responsibility, the fear, the indecision, but mostly I swore for having been implicated by timing and curiosity. "Shit, now what?"

I was in town for a few months as an employee of The Red Cross, to help
the local chapter initiate their disaster relief organization. You would expect
someone of this background, trained to handle disaster, to be a calm, analytical
thinker, someone who would have gone back to the car where their cell phone
rested on the passenger seat, and called 911.

But I was apparently influenced by the immediacy of the circumstance so greatly
that I clambered down the rocky slope hands and feet. The car was further
down and a more difficult scramble than I had anticipated. I passed beyond
the influence of my car above, still running, to hear that the car below was not
running. I had passed a hubcap on my way down and then a muffler. I felt like
my muffler was about to fall off as will; my shins were taking a bruising, my
hands scuffed and full of stickers.

The car was face-planted against a big pine tree. I could detect a wisp of smoke
or steam rising from it. I figured someone had to be in there because the doors
were not open, but because I heard nothing my assumptions were on the
dark side.

How did I find myself involved in this yet another intersection of emergency?
Stumbling into a robbery in progress, walking behind an old woman on a busy
street whose purse was snatched, dogs hit by cars, lost children, a coup d'état in
Latin America— seems I was fated for these unfortunate conjunctures, and my
history of reaction hadn't been that stellar.

I vowed after all of these to be better prepared, but dismissed any action of
preparation based on odds. What are the chances lightening is going to strike the
same fool twice?

A couple of tools would have been appreciated, a flashlight, my cell phone, latex
gloves, all in my car up above. I saw as I approached that the car was a newer
model Mercedes. It was definitely smoke, not steam, escaping from the crunched
hood.

I saw the lady slumped in her seat, head resting on shoulder, motionless, but my
attempt to open the door was unsuccessful. Jesus, I thought, what if she is locked
inside this smoking bomb? As I circled around the pine tree, I could see the front
of the car was flattened but good; the impact must have been dramatic. Smoke
was really boiling out now, heightening my anxiety.

The passenger door swung open easily. I crawled across the seat and rested my fingers on her carotid artery. There was a pulse and I could hear her shallow, bubbling breath. I felt the thick, sticky blood on my hand; however it was too dark to see the extent of her injuries.

The seatbelt had restrained her, preventing a collision with the windshield, but her head had apparently bounced off the steering wheel. With an impact as great as this one appeared to be, she likely had incurred neck or spinal injury. She was unconscious.

I was suffering minor shock myself as I crouched on the seat weighing my options. Should I struggle back up to my car and call for help or risk further injury to her by pulling her out the passenger door and away from the car. These were decisions that I didn't imagine during Red Cross first aid/CPR training.

The smoke was intensifying, flooding into the car. Its acrid electrical stink was burning my eyes. I considered the liability of leaving her with permanent spinal paralysis by dragging her out of the car; understood this dilemma for first responders. All of this was compounded by the fact I am African-American in a very white and conservative area of the state. This is another level of consideration people of color must contend with when involving themselves in this country.

Her inhaling this caustic smoke and the potential for fire were too great to chance, I assessed.

"Shit, why me?" I cursed as I unlatched her seat belt.

As gently as possible I linked an arm under her arm, supported her head with my other hand, and extricated her from behind the wheel, easing her to the door. I positioned my body so when I pulled her out of the car she would fall on me rather than the rocks. She wasn't a large woman, thank God. Again, I supported her head and drug her by the collar of her coat 30-40 feet into the trees imagining her spinal cord rasping against jagged vertebrae as I pulled her across the forest floor.

I rolled her on her side in a flat grassy area, her head resting on her arm. I couldn't see her injuries and worried about blood running down her throat interfering with her breathing. Aided by adrenalin—that luckily blocked too much analysis—I scrabbled back up the steep slope to my car and called 911.

I waited above for the EMT's, wiping my bloody hands on my clothes obsessively. They came: state patrol, two fire trucks and ambulance, a parade of flashing lights and sirens piercing a black moonless night.

By the time I had answered all the official questions, they had hauled the stretcher up to the road. The best I could tell as they stuffed her into the ambulance was she was a middle-aged woman and her face was pretty messed up. I returned to my hotel and couldn't sleep.

I waited two days before curiosity more than concern lead me to the hospital. I had no name to ask for so I described the accident and the time. It took awhile, but we identified her as Millie Stuart. She was stable, but with a family only guest list. I asked the nurse to tell her I was the guy who had drug her across the rocks and she consented to allow me an audience.

She looked at me with anesthetic eyes as I introduced myself and she extended a hand with an IV tube attached to it, "Millie, and thank you, thank you. How do I repay you?"

"That's silly, I'm just glad you are okay."

"How about I give you my car?" A smile broke from her bruised, puffy, black-eyed and bandaged face. I couldn't decide what her normal face might look like, it was so misshapen.

We had a short, but interesting conversation. Her sense of humor infiltrated the pain and her self-consciousness cancelled any prejudice she might have held for minorities.

"How grotesque I must look!"

She had been angry at her husband, had a few drinks and was driving from the ranch to spend the night with her sister in town. Traveling too fast, she lost control and went over the brink.

When the nurse came to shoo me out, Millie extended her hand again and asked if I'd pay her another visit; she'd be there a few more days and our conversation, our laughing at ourselves, had made her feel better. I considered not visiting again, letting things fade out on a good note, but I too had enjoyed our conversation, her humor and pluck, and I sensed a loneliness in her.

When I returned the next day her husband was just leaving. He looked prosperous, over-weight and spongy, as prosperous people often do; wearing jeans, boots and an expensive western jacket. His hands looked white and soft; somebody else was doing the ranch work I thought.

"Marshall Stuart" He nodded, "Thanks for helping Millie."

"Eshone Jimenez," I responded offering my hand.

He didn't take it and said, "Pretty good English. You're the first black Mexican I've seen."

"Cuban, sir, 3rd generation American. My grandfather fought as a member of the 25th Infantry Regiment of the Buffalo Soldiers alongside Teddy Roosevelt in 1898 at San Juan Hill in Cuba during the Spanish-American War."

He took his checkbook out of his jacket pocket. "I suppose you want something?"

"No, sir," I said with hint of too much defiance, "I'm just pleased that Millie is okay and improving."

"Hump! I don't suppose you resisted any of this government's handouts. What are you doing here?"

"No more than you, sir. I am here with the Red Cross helping organize their disaster relief services."

"With big government funding." His last words as he walked out not saying good bye to Millie.

"Marshall is upset with my crashing the car and, of course, Obama's re-election. He can be very charming. We are still in a state of disbelief that Mitt didn't win.

You obviously voted for Obama, so you can't imagine our disappointment." She was visibly uncomfortable, as was I. I was about to leave when she continued, "Stuart doesn't even speak to my sister because of her Obama support. She's the only person we know who didn't vote for Romney."

"Birds of a feather…"

"True, birds of a feather. You work for a service organization so, of course, you support big government unlike people in business."

"Well, yes, we generally agree that a more equitable sharing of wealth and resources would be a good thing, help preserve the middle class and relieve suffering of the poor and possibly prevent an economic revolution."

"Marshall and his cronies are fond of quoting Nobel economist Milton Friedman, 'The more money in the pockets of the wealthy, the better off the poor.'"

"Yes, of course, trickle down, a throwback to the Reagan 80"s. Well, Millie, I'll go now and wish you a quick recovery."

"You're getting a little worked up, aren't you? Poor Marshall, he can't stand being on the losing side. Personally, I don't give a hoot, but Marshall is just a neurotic basket case. He's so polarized. He used to be such a gentleman, but he's let his health go, gotten fat, has diabetes and he's impotent. He's forgotten how to enjoy life. We must be empathetic though. He is not a product of himself, but of the closed world he has never escaped. He was born here and other than Canada has not left this country. He is isolated in his information; it all comes from Fox News and his Catholic faith has him subservient to ecumenical dictates. Change is not in the cards."

"But, please, Eshone, don't be upset with me over something as silly as politics and understand you are the first black person I have known. Dare I be seen with you? Personally, it would feel good for me to walk downtown with you, but as bad as that might go for me, it would go worse for you, and you have work to do here. However, I would like you to meet my sister. When I get out of here I will give you a call and we'll have you over to her house for dinner. What do you say?"

When I met Millie at her sister's house I hardly recognized her with her tight Wrangler jeans, boots, and sassy western shirt. Even with the black eyes and bandages she had a pretty face and struck quite an attractive figure.

Her sister was considerably younger, going through a divorce and ready to 'get out of this Republican town,' as she put it. We had a surprisingly provocative conversation, Millie asking probing questions and listening with an open mind. She shared her attempt to accept how life had laid out the dominoes differently than she had expected.

"Status quo is difficult to escape, like swimming at great risk from an island of plenty and discontentment across uncharted water to the possibility of another island that may be better, or maybe not. You have to be pretty fed up to make that plunge. I'm almost to that point. Stuart is such a controlling man, afraid of losing what he's accumulated, bitter and defensive. I don't see much sunshine ahead."

As I left that night she revisited the need to repay me for having helped her. "You rode in on your black horse, drug me from the burning car and now you are making me question whether I voted for the wrong candidate."

It was then that Millie invited me out to the ranch to ride. Her stiffness from the accident was beginning to abate and she was ready to get back in the saddle. I asked if that might not just upset Marshall more and she retorted, "It's my ranch too!"

She met me at her sister's house that next weekend in her new vehicle, a beat up Ford F-150 pickup, wearing her cowgirl outfit topped with a white Stetson.

"You look good driving this pickup!"

"Thank you, Mr. Detroit, and you look like you just stepped out of an L.L.Bean catalogue with those hiking boots and fleece ready for a western adventure."

"This western adventure I am about to have—I am being pretty trusting here—how could this go wrong?"

"Can't, I've got your back."

"Tell me about 'The Ranch.'"

"Fourth generation Stuart Flying Fox Ranch. Primarily a cow and calf operation; 3,000 acres and 4 sections of leased BLM land. We still breed quarter horses, but at one time Marshall and his father raised rodeo stock: broncs, bulls, etc., big business. I met Marshall at the Edmonton Stampede. I was a young barrel racer, all about rodeo then and he was a player in that scene as one of the major stock providers."

"You're Canadian?"

"Yes."

"Don't think of Canadians as cowboys."

"Why not?"

"Probably because I grew up in Detroit."

"City boy!" She smiled.

"Suburb boy, really. My parents were both teachers so we weren't poor Detroit. Our cowboy experience was limited to TV and movies."

"Well, you are in the heart of it now, whatever it has become."

"And it fascinates me. It is a sub-culture I stand outside of and peer into with interest. When you walked into your sister's the other day all decked out in your wranglers and hat, you had my full attention."

"You didn't mention the train wreck of a face."

"Hey, it looks like a face at least. When I visited you in the hospital it was more of a beachball."

"Thank you. I think that was complimentary, or maybe just a positive spin." She laughed. "While we're on faces, as a big man you have a pretty face. Oh, I hope you're not embarrassed by that. I meant it as a compliment."

"I've been told that before, that I am pretty. I don't know what the stock value of being pretty is for a man. It must be this pudgy little nose I came out with."

"No, baby, it's those gorgeous big eyes and those eyelashes. I got to tell you any woman not getting a little heart zing from those must be a lesbian and maybe them too. Those are doll eyelashes."

"Okay, I will buy stock in that compliment. Thank you. How will this black face, doll eyelashes or not, work out on the ranch?"

"Oh, don't worry about it. Ignorant people's ignorance comes from lack of experience and they will always judge."

"Are you judging?"

"Oh, sure, but it is close to the surface for me, and I have the 'stay-open-minded' chat with myself often. I see you as a black man, but I don't think of you as a black man. My son…"

"You have a child?"

"Why does that surprise you?"

"You haven't mentioned him."

"He's 23, a student at ASU and a pea in the pod with his father, almost Aryan in his bigotry. Don't get me wrong, he's good to his mother, but doesn't give women much truck. I just hope this university experience will broaden his scope a bit, although I haven't seen it yet."

"How old are you? I can't believe you have a 23 year old kid."

"Aren't you sweet. How old do you think I am?"

"Now you've trapped me. My mom suggested I always deduct five years from my estimate in such circumstances. 45!"

"All right, I like your mother. I am 53. You see these sprays of gray hair escaping my hat? I like those. They are bullet marks on my wisdom resume. Marshall feels I have become too unpredictable, too forward in expressing myself, no longer the trophy cowgirl, quiet and without opinion, on his arm. I figure I have some life catching-up to do, and I am moving forward with it."

"What's that life catching-up going to look like?"

"I've already explained to Marshall I am going back to school, which means leaving here. I'm going to travel; I am going to live through my heart, not my head for the remainder."

"Wow, I am happy for you. Those kinds of transitions take courage, but be prepared for there to be bodies left lying in the road, expendables. Is you're bringing a black man out to the ranch to ride a piece of the new look? Hope I'm not the guy lying in the road when the dust settles."

I watched the landscape change as we drove down into the desert; Joshua trees, juniper, cactus, green riparian ribbons of cottonwood and ash along the creeks, pink granite boulders backlit by an unblemished blue sky.

"Here we are!" She announced as we pulled through an over-arching gate, down a long lane bordered by white fencing, and up to a huge barn with surrounding paddocks. A big pond surrounded by weeping willow trees separated the barn from a large, stylish house. It didn't look like the desert here. More outbuildings were scattered about and farm equipment. An old gray-muzzled black lab was the first to greet us, tail in an excited wag.

"I kind of hate to tell you what the dog's name is."

"Go ahead, I am prepared."

"Nigger!"

"Perfect. I will just call him 'boy,' if he doesn't mind. And who is this coming out of the barn?" A real-deal cowboy emerged from the darkness of the gaping barn entrance.

"This would be Flint. He manages the horse operation here at the Flying Fuck…excuse me, please. That was in poor taste. This is what my sister and I jokingly call the Stuart Flying Fox Ranch."

"Morning, Miss Millie." Flint is a weathered looking 40 something wiry little man. He was talking to Millie, but looked somewhat quizzically at me.

"Flint, this is Eshone." Flint extended a gloved hand through the window and we shook.

"Guess we owe you a 'thank you' for pulling our little lady out of the wreck."

"Flint, Eshone and I are going to ride. I will get Sadie ready; could you maybe saddle the sorrel?"

"I don't know about using the boss's horse, Miss Millie."

"Well, Marshall never rides him and he's about as gentle an animal as we have."

"Ride before?" Flint looked at me smiling.

"Never."

"Didn't figure you people would have much experience on horses. Okay, I'll get the old sorrel ready."

We walked into the barn. The wonderful warm smell of horses, alfalfa, and leather greeted me. It was clean and voluminous, tack hung neatly next to each stall. Only a quarter of the stalls held horses, all beautiful, fit looking animals.

"Long drink of water, ain't ya?" Flint eyed me top to bottom. "Basketball boy I bet."

"Yes, Flint, I've played some ball and as you're assuming, this is a brand new experience for me. Millie tells me you're the horse manager and that you know horses about as well as anyone can. I'm always impressed with that kind of expertise. And, since we've got stereotypes swirling around the barn, I imagine you were on a horse before you could walk?"

"What the hell's a stereotype?"

"You know, the assumptions we make about folks looking in from the outside. Do you use snuff?"

"I do!"

"Perfect. I would love to try some of that if I could."

"You wanna try snuff?"

"Yeah, why not, broaden my horizons; try on as many experiences as I can during my day on the ranch."

Flint pulled a can of Copenhagen out of his rear pocket and popped the lid. "Pinch abit and stuff it under your lip. Don't think about where your fingers have been when you do it." He produced a hardy laugh, accentuating the bulge under his bottom lip.

"You worry about it?"

"Never do!"

I felt we had broken some ice with our little tobacco exchange. I poked a small pinch under my lip and went off with Millie to saddle her buttermilk mare, Sadie.

Millie was efficient and smooth; had saddled a horse hundreds of times. She explained what she was doing as she worked. "We use a hackamore with Marshall's sorrel rather than a bridle. He is old and has a soft mouth, so you lose some control. But, not to worry—his eyesight is weak so he'll stick with Sadie." She looked up at me as she tightened Sadie's saddle cinch. You must always tighten the cinch a second time or you and the saddle might roll right off." And finally, "Expect to be a little sore after a few hours in the saddle."

She was a natural in the saddle, relaxed and smooth, as though one with Sadie. We left the green cool of the pasture, passed through a gate and out onto sandy desert trails. The sorrel responded to whatever gait Millie took Sadie to.

When Millie saw I was doing fine at a walk she sped up to a trot, bouncy and uncomfortable for me. She changed her saddle posture for the trot, rose up on her legs more, her trim hips rising above the back of the saddle in cadence, breasts rising and falling appealingly. The canter was more rhythmic, but faster and I had both hands on the saddle horn feeling very vulnerable. She broke into a gallop for a short sprint. The gallop is the fastest gait, a dead run. She leaned forward, hands far in front of her body, and seemingly supported her body off the saddle with her legs. I would have loved to have been able to watch her and Sadie thundering along that trail from the safety of the earth, but I was clinging to the sorrel's mane, totally focused on not falling. My reins, the steering wheel of this horse, laid useless across the saddle horn. I was completely out of control; this horse was taking no direction from me anyway.

As we walked the horses back toward the barn I suggested that women look more natural on a horse than a man, and teenaged girls seem universally to pass through a stage of horse mania.

"Well, think about the anatomy of the genders," she reasoned with me, "spreading your legs across a saddle comes easier to a female, and with 1200 pounds of muscle moving rhythmically under a leather saddle you might be able to imagine there is a physical gratification present."

It did indeed make sense.

Nothing short of rigor mortis had assailed my butt by the time we had returned to the sister's house. "Millie, I thought you said I might be a little sore? I can hardly move and all this time I thought cowboys walked like they had shit in their pants because of the boots."

Millie was having a good laugh at my expense. "Come on in cowboy, we'll get you some ibuprofen."

"No, I need something stronger. This is no over-the-counter soreness. I think I'm injured!"

There was a note on the refrigerator from her sister:

Millie, there's a bottle of Page Springs Chardonnay in the fridge for you. The real estate guy is coming to put signs up tomorrow at 10; could you be here to leave him the key? I will see you in a few weeks. Thanks, I love you, Sidra.

"Guess we better drink that wine in celebration of your new cowboy status, and we will need to think about getting you dressed correctly for it."

"What's in it for me?"

"How Republican of you to ask that." She smiled and took a tug off the bottle of wine.

"I guess this town is rubbing off on me."

"Well, they wouldn't want you rubbing off on them." She handed me the bottle. "There are no glasses left in the house; we'll have to share this like a couple of Democrats."

"Do you think my cowboy hat should be white or black?" I asked wiping wine from my lips with a shirt sleeve.

"White hats come with too much talk and bravado. I think the black hat is your best choice; it comes with some license to deviate. I'm getting me one."

"And the shirt, I want a western shirt like yours, with snaps!"

"You like snaps?"

"I like snaps!"

With a deviant smile she dug her shirt tail out of those tight Wranglers and with two hands, pop, pop, pop, bottom to top, I waited for the pause, but she didn't stop.

"How Democratic of you!" I said as I stepped inside her invitation.

YOUTH:

COMING OF AGE ON THE RESERVATION

Neccos

Written in:

Buenos Aires, Argentina

Can you pee across the ditch, Bernard?

Course I can see across the ditch, I can see all the way to tomorrow, I just can't hear across the damned ditch.

No, I said can you PEE across the ditch?

Why would I if I can pee on this side?

I can pee across the ditch.

Nope.

Want to see me?

Well, it's not something I've been holdin' out for in this life, but I suspect I'm going to get to anyway.

Carl Longernecker and I had contests all the time. He could run faster than I, hold his breath longer, lift heavier stuff, but I could out-pee him. I could pee cursive to M in the snow, and although he was ten too he couldn't even do cursive and I could pee way farther than he could, so I was pretty sure I could pee across the ditch. I prepared myself; got a good pressure built up then thrust myself forward and let her fly. The stream looked certain to pass over the ditch with dirt to spare, but the wind sprung up rustling that stream of piss and carried it back toward Bernard. He ducked away from the mist and fished his handkerchief out of hind pocket in the same motion.

When he came up he was in the throws of a full laughing fit. High-pitched, uncontrollable cackles; hands on his knees and his hat lying upside down on the road. He laughed like a desert dog drinks. The joy was splashing out of his action, contagious; it got on me and I started laughing and soon was on my back on the road, doubled-up like I was having an appendicitis attack. He was raising and lowering his hands like a Holy Roller on Sunday, which made me laugh harder. The value of a good memory and a good laugh cannot be overestimated. You come out of one exhausted and cleansed and ready for some Neccos.

Asking yourself how you got to be the way you are is like wondering what rivers are represented in a handful of ocean water.

Fortunately as you get older, when you are more inclined to ask, the answer is more inclined to reveal itself, however gradually, like a Polaroid picture evolving through a blurry swirl into a recognizable image. That image appears to me as my maternal grandfather, Charles Stark.

When I look at these broad, work-sore hands of mine, the blackened fingernails and scuffed knuckles, I see Papa Charles. When I see in the mirror the ridged crown on my bald head, I'm looking at my grandfather. When I investigate why I've just diverted a question about myself for the discomfort it brings, I'm lead directly to his memory.

My image of Papa Charles is sketched from a scrapbook of memories I compiled during the months I spent with my grandparents during the summer of my tenth year. That scrapbook is full of sights, sounds and smells that tempt my nostalgia; none more enticing than his old red pickup truck that transports me back, like a guarantee, to that summer of 1955.

It was the first truck built after World War II and as much a military tank as a civilian vehicle; prone to smoke, noise and mass. Slamming one of the massive doors of that pickup set off a metallic peal of thunder more damaging to tender ears than profanity.

In my smallness it was huge and a rough road would have me bouncing around the cab. Seat and belt had not been used in conjunction with each other yet. My grandfather's pipe would be clenched between his teeth filling the cab with a blue acrid haze of second-hand cancer. Papa Charles steering with both hands in exaggerated swings, back and forth, so one would have expected that old truck to be lurching from side to side like a carnival ride, but with a steering mechanism as loose as next year's overalls it moved off, through its own smoke, straight and true, in his happy grasp.

Those hands were integral to his communication, as though he were presenting a lecture to the deaf. The hands were integrated into his every action, even if it were what we might consider a manually non-participatory verb like thinking; such as the time he knocked the table lamp to the
floor that sat on the smoking stand by his easy chair. Lottie, my grandmother, who weighed not much more than that lamp and therefore was justifiably unnerved, was so agitated by the crash she spoke out in her censorious cloudy day manner:

It's little wonder, Charlotte Cox, (her maiden name) *your nerves are shattered and the elegant grace that drew suitors from as far as Muckleton have been bullied into an inflicted anxiety that has you as brittle as a winter stick.*

Her eyes didn't follow the dispensation of her words as they were helping her bony hands repair the resulting dropped crochet stitch.

Papa Charles, a perpetual defendant in 'Lottie's' court, countered in his pseudo-apologetic way:

I was thinking about setting the hook on those fussy whitefish Boy and I were pulling out of the Tieton River yesterday.

Boy was me.

I was spending some summer time with my grandparents while my father, a dour work-brittle man and modestly unsuccessful farmer, was sick. We—my father, mother, older sister and I—had been living in a small clapboard structure my father built with lumber remaining after the construction of a fine barn, on eighty acres of leased Yakima Indian Nation land. It was good for me to have wide open spaces to roam, farm responsibilities to assume, and a dog, Elmer, for a companion, but it wasn't this good for my sister who was isolated from her social world or for my mother who had to drive fifty miles a day to work in the office of a fruit warehouse.

My father was one of those men of few words who let his dour, presbyterian work ethic speak for him. He set impossible goals then would go to any necessary effort to meet them. He was awake at light and asleep at dark and took what joy he received from his work; work which consumed his physical and directed his mental. He didn't rest and if he had to go to town on errands he certainly didn't dawdle at the coffeeshop or waste precious time with preventative medicine or dentistry. He chose to ignore the aches and pains that came with hard work and aging, so it must have been an awful pain in his gut that convinced him to let my mother take him to the doctor. The pain was latent pancreatic cancer and when he was admitted into the hospital it was only the third time in his life he'd been there; the other two the birth of his children. He never left.

I was, at ten years of age, in the backseat of the adult world, hearing some and understanding less of the conversation carried on before me. I knew my father was sick, but I had been sick before and always sprang back in a few days, hungry and ready to wrestle. The new medical vocabulary alone was enough to leave me confused as a bird at the window, so I was not aware of the seriousness of his condition.

I saw this visit to my grandparents as a new adventure, an opportunity to go to work with Papa Charles and sleep on the back porch; a room of my own after years of sharing with my sister.

Old and weatherworn, my grandparent's house had once been the principal residence of a large farm. That farmhouse sat in a row of modest houses on a modest street with modest automobiles parked along it. A grand and gnarled walnut tree in the front yard distinguished it, gathered your eyes upon turning down their block and delivered them to Grandmother Lottie's flowerbeds that adorned it; a colorful dress on an old woman.

The inside of her house possessed a hidden form of order that the dense clutter of trinketry and doilies sat in front of like too many words obscure an idea. Every chair, couch and table wore a doily that she had crocheted. Each evening Papa Charles retired to his easy chair and removed the many doilies that had covered the dark sebaceous stain where he rested his bald pate and where there were hundreds of small burn holes from his constant fiddling with hot ash in the bowl of his pipe. That old chair was his sole refuge in her domain and she knew it wasn't going anywhere so she tolerated it, covering it with doilies every morning when he left for work.

It was Lottie's house and all ways there were her ways right down to the detailed protocol of how I excused myself from the table and how my shoes sat together like tired oxen where I took them off at her door.

Lottie was a little thing—stood not much above me in her heeled black lace-ups and weighed less than a box of books. The pictures on the wall suggested she had been a beautiful young woman, but always frail; a frailty she employed for a special compensation she expected from everyone.

Papa Charles called her his pretty little bird and tended to her challenges with a cheerful responsibility. My father called her 'that banty brood hen,' putting the best construction on a situation he'd always come up short on. In her home we were all humble passengers in a vehicle that she alone guided. In the outside world she didn't drive, in truth seldom left the port anchoring of her home. If she had driven, there would have been a blue handicapped sticker hanging from her mirror—that pass to special privileges so often abused by old ladies with nothing wrong with them other than their shoes hurt their feet or they can't see over the steering wheel of their Oldsmobile.

Grandmother Lottie's nerves—Papa Charles said she had hurry sickness— disqualified me from spending anymore than minimal time alone with her. This meant I was the exclusive ward of Papa Charles, germinating some of the finest memories of my childhood.

As a diversion engineer for the Rosa reclamation project, Papa Charles was responsible for allocating irrigation water to the orchards that spread across the valley like green hair on a brown dog. Through the middle of the valley ran the canal—the ditch he called it—a deep and wide man made river. Along its dikes was his office.

Papa Charles anointed Bernard and me 'associate ditch riders'—water gods to the orchardists. We might as well have been a couple of leading men the way the orchardists treated us. Papa Charles hadn't paid for a cup of coffee in eight years.

The Hop Inn Café consisted of a counter and twelve swivel stools occupied by men wearing caps with fertilizer logos, and Papa Charles was there at least once a day. A couple of stools would come vacant upon our entry and a cup of coffee and glass of milk would arrive on the counter before I could pull myself up on the stool.

Vivian, with orange hair and a cigarette smoldering in a nearby ashtray, managed that counter the way Van Cliburn might have played the Flight of the Bumblebee on the piano; up and down that counter never spending long with any one customer, but engaging them all.

Her smoker's cough sounded like someone shaking a tin bucket with a handful of gravel and her apron read, 'If I ain't happy, you ain't happy.'

She would produce a leather dice cup from under the counter and everyone would take their turn rolling the dice playing some homespun game that brought shouts and groans to determine who was buying Papa Charles' coffee.

He would tip his skinny brimmed work hat far back on his head—the place he kept it when he wasn't wearing it—and revel in the camaraderie. The conversations, loud and laughy, were a foreign language of fruit production, price projections and spray applications. Papa Charles, as though speaking yet another language, interpreted every word with his perpetually busy hands, a cup of coffee in one, his pipe in the other.

The khaki shirt with sleeves rolled up past the elbow was as ubiquitous as the pipe protruding out the side of his mouth. As a sound sleep is the servant of a good morning, Papa Charles' slippers served his feet. He had a sturdy pair for inside the house and a sturdier pair he wore everywhere else.

Why you wearing your slippers Papa Charles?

Boy, if a man's feet aren't comfortable his work is going to suffer. Let me explain to you; Milton, my little brother, got to wear all the clothes I outgrew, and he was always bigger than me. His feet hurt so in my hand-me-down boots that he'd only do work he could reach from where he was standing and that isn't much when you're bucking bales of hay. You know what they say about a man with big feet don't you?

And I would say no I don't, which along with 'Nuh Uhn' and 'Did Not' was pretty much my pat answer to every question aimed my way. That came with having an accusatory older sister,

Boy has his church shoes on Mom!

'No, I don't!' And so on.

Well, he'd give some obscure, but interesting exposé about men with big feet that I didn't understand, both his hands flailing in full interpretation, disengaged from the wheel of the moving pickup, and then he'd laugh like he did with his pipe clenched in his teeth.

Papa Charles was a man formed outside the mold of a father. He was shaped by what he saw from a distance: fathers of his friends, suitors to his sister, men he watched in church. He tried on the personas of these men: rugged, tough, good timers, but in the end he became what nature had written out for him: cheerful and gregarious with a strong compliment of kindness, empathy and appreciation for the lot of women. He was, in the end, the by-product of a loving and strong mother.

Underneath the deep and healthy shine of a good man boiled a cauldron of molten insecurity— the settlement of not having a father. A father, an involved father, has always been the strong arms of encouragement, the absolute voice of discipline, the fundamental model for how a man greets another man, loves a woman, cares for his tools, expresses his weaknesses, all of which constitute the matriculation of maturity.

So he became his own intention; a complete and successful meal of a man.

He employed humor as a deflection for the discomfort of small talk. Learning the skill of interview, he used the question as a distraction to draw attention away from himself, responding with a justaudible voice underneath the rubble of his childhood telling him his opinion was not cogent, that nobody was really listening.

Like a hymn sung over and over in church, his mother's often-recited words of relationship rose regularly to the surface of his consciousness: never leave a kind thought unoffered and honesty and love begin with yourself.

Papa Charles knew the seriousness of my father's illness, that the cancer in his guts would kill him. He understood he would have to rise above his own limitations and desires to fill that void in my life. Like pulling open that heavy door of the church Lottie made him attend, it was difficult for him to open those conversations with me.

As with any chat, his hands would have to be involved, if not swinging the big steering wheel then fiddling with something, attempting to put a crease in his hat that had been creased too many times in too many places to hold any intentional crease, let alone water. If asked, that hat would have long ago quit calling itself a hat, but rather something available to keep his hands busy.

My mother didn't tell me for two days that my father had died. Papa Charles explained to me that when he was 12 he had to help his ma take care of his little brothers while his father was laying on the bed upstairs sick from the accident.

Ma wasn't talking much, he said, *her face was red and swollen and she kept giving hard hugs, like to squeeze the juice out of us.*

What accident? I asked.

He was run over by a wagon.

A wagon? That won't kill ya, Papa Charles.

I'm not talking about your Radio Flyer, Boy. This was a horse-drawn hay wagon. Horses were spooked by a stray dog. He toppled off; wheel rolled over him and crushed him. I suppose it was my fault.

Why?

Well, I fed that stray dog against my parents' wishes and of course he stuck around. The horses didn't know him. They spooked, you know; he frightened them and they bolted or something.

He went on, talking more than I had ever heard him talk,

My ma told me my father was upstairs in his room and that I shouldn't disturb him. After a few days I went upstairs to see him anyway, but he wasn't there. I ran down stairs to tell my ma that he'd snuck off. That's when she told me my father was dead.

The little ones started crying, but I didn't cry. I got angry. I was angry at my father for dying, at ma for not telling me and I was angry at that stray dog. Mostly, I was angry at myself for not chasing that dog off.

You mad at me?

No, Boy, I'm not mad at anybody anymore, but I decided after that I had to take care of my ma, the little fellas, the wife and children I'd have someday. Now your dad has died and you have inherited that responsibility.

What's inherit mean?

It's a gift you get from your folks when they're gone.

You mean like a Christmas present?

No, more like a very important job they assign you.

Well, I already have my pockets full of chores. I've gotta feed Elmer, take out the trash, milk Bessie, fetch the mail, feed the chickens, gather the eggs, dry the dishes…

Yep, you got your hands full. I swam that river of guilt back and forth on the verge of sinking and drowning. What finally drew me to shore was that needy stray dog who didn't know he'd done wrong, but was counting on me. I started to see how the world didn't always line up in my favor and if I could take the bad along with the good the good, it was going to be worth more.

I didn't know what he was talking about and he was staring out the window like he was watching something so I didn't know if he was even talking to me. He looked real sad and I felt sorry for him. I was hoping real hard he wasn't gong to start crying, so I leaned over and rested my head against his shoulder.

Sorry Papa Charles, I lost all those fish we caught the other day.

No, Boy, you did great. He put his arm around me and looked down smiling the best he could without his pipe falling out of his mouth. He looked like he was glad he was done talking about whatever it was he had been talking about.

I saw how you handled yourself when you went down crossing the river with that creel heavy with white fish. It was quite the sight; it filling up with water and carrying you down stream like a parachute. You bounced over the rocks, all the while trying to save our supper. You're a good one, Boy, except you piss too close to the house.

He squeezed my shoulder, *I would have come in to get you, but I had my favorite pipe in my hand. Let's keep it our secret though. It would upset your grandmother.*

Pretty much everything upset Lottie.

When she got upset and her little violin voice would get loud and screechy it could break windows. Avoiding that voice was reason enough not to upset her, but my being there disrupted her routine enough that she was upset pretty much all the time.

She would sit on the very edge of a chair, her feet together under her knees, like you sit when you're in trouble at school. She'd set that big black handbag on top of her knees and rest both hands on the clasp, open and close, open and close, click, click, click, and I would cringe just anticipating the screeching to begin. This was the same bag she would carry around the house with the strap draped over the crook of her arm. When she wasn't upset she kept her handbag in the refrigerator; 'to keep it fresh,' she told me.

Another way we knew when Lottie was upset was when she started pulling her hankie out of the sleeve of her dress and tucking it back in. One day when Papa Charles and I came home I saw Lottie's friend, Mame Ursherwood's car parked in the alley. Whenever Mame Ursherwood came to visit she'd knock the garbage can over in the alley. She was pretty much blind, I think, and wore thick glasses—coke bottles Papa Charles called them—that made her eyes look like bow and arrow targets. She had to keep her nose wrinkled in order to hold those heavy glasses on her face and that would raise her lip so her teeth were always showing. It made talking to Mame very difficult with the target eyes and little rodent mouth.

Well, when we got home that day I had to pee, but Papa Charles told me to stop peeing outside 'cause it upset Lottie. I went into the house to use the bathroom and had to walk between Mame's and Lottie's conversation. Mame was leaning way into the conversation trying to see better and Lottie was sitting on the edge of her chair tucking and untucking that hankie in her sleeve. I stopped a moment to hear what this upsetting conversation was about. It turns out they weren't talking to each other. Lottie was complaining about Mrs. Doak's grandson next door flipping cigarette butts onto her lawn and Mame was complaining about car insurance. Neither Mame or Lottie were listening to the other. They were like two little kids in a sandbox playing along next to somebody else.

Skippy, Lottie screeched, *you're standing in the middle of our conversation!*

She called me Johnny or Skippy, her other grandsons' names, because I was the third one born and three of anything is a lot to remember.

I disturbed the calm of Papa Charles's and Lottie's day. One afternoon he said to me: *Boy, you're making your grandmother nervous which doesn't work to my benefit, so why don't you go out back and dig a hole. Let me know when you're done and we'll find something to throw in it.*

I spent a lot of time in the backyard, happily. Living on an isolated farm deep on the Yakima Indian Reservation had prepared me to be inventive in solitude. There was a definitive number of times you can throw a rock left handed at a little garage window with your eyes closed before you hit it. I was testing out what my southpaw friend Carl Longernecker had said about me not being able to hit the broad side of a barn left handed. Well, I could. The sound was loud and satisfying, like, well like hitting the side of a barn with a rock. There was a little window I never imagined I'd hit, but I hit that too. Papa Charles wasn't mad, but said let's keep this our little secret.

Lottie never came out to the garage; this was Papa Charles's hideout—'the dog house'—he called it, where he kept his beloved tools. The garage was off-limits to me; too much 'sharp and heavy' he said. It fascinated me, as all off-limits

did, and I found I could squeeze through the gap of the big sliding door. It
was dark and smelled like grease, which has always held some odd attraction
for me. It smelled like grease because there were greasy things in there and if I
wasn't real careful that grease would get on me and I would be found out. Once
while attempting to investigate the contents of a coffee can on a high shelf I got
smudged a good one. That's what Lottie called any stain or soil on me or my
clothes; a smudge. So I had to come up with an excuse for the grease smudge on
my pants. I wiggled underneath my grandparent's Oldsmobile and waited until
Lottie called me into dinner. I emerged from under the car smudged up
real good.

What are your doing? She asked in her screeching accusatory manner,
accentuating the word 'doing' like I was running through church naked.

What do you want to do when you are big, Boy? Papa Charles asked me one day
while driving out to the ditch.

Play baseball for the Dodgers.

Well, let that dream be your stray dog, his hands steering furiously. *I was going to
be a doctor and not let anyone die, but that was silly wasn't it? Every living thing
has to die, your parents and me, and someday way off, you too. I told my brothers
and friends that I was going to be a doctor so they started calling me Doc. It is a
hard pill to swallow that they still call me Doc and I'm not one. Probably best to say
what you'd like to do, not what you're going to do; give yourself a little wiggle room.
Life will float you, but its depths are full of sharks. You understand what I'm
saying, Boy?*

I'd say, yes sir, like I always did so he wouldn't say it all again, but I didn't
understand, sharks and pills. I did know I was hungry though, and I was hoping
we would see Bernard, Papa Charles's ditch rider buddy, because he always had
Neccos in his pocket.

Bernard was African-American. People didn't call him that then; they called him
a Negro. Papa Charles called him, my friend Bernard. Bernard couldn't go to the
Hop Inn Café, which couldn't have been too great of a disappointment to him

since the Hop Inn was loud and crowded and he was a solitary man. He lived alone with his dog, Oklahoma, and was hard of hearing.

He can't hear all the way to where he's standing, Papa Charles told me; *you have to move within arm's length to communicate.*

Bernard stood away from a conversation. Maybe it was a habit he learned as a little black kid growing up back in the day. Maybe it was because most of his conversations were with Papa Charles and he didn't want to get clipped on the nose by those constantly flailing hands.

When I first met Bernard I was with Papa Charles in his pickup. We had just arrived at the power house on the ditch and Bernard was there.

I don't know, Charles, which is givin' out more smoke, Bernard said, *this truck or that cockamamie pipe of yours, but I'm grateful for both 'cause it's a whole lot easier to take this conversation serious not havin' to see that worn-out face you bring to it.*

Papa Charles laughed his FDR laugh; teeth clenching on his pipe. *Here, Bernard let me turn this engine off.*

Say, you got the Injun cough? Bernard never said, 'what' or asked you to repeat what he didn't hear. He'd just approximate what he thought you said and repeat it back to you for validation.

Papa Charles turned to me raising the level of his normal soft voice, *Bernard's hard of hearing, Boy.*

Charles is a bit hard of listening, Bernard retorted and reached a long bony black hand into the truck toward me. *I'm Bernard.* And he shook my hand like he was driving nails.

This is my grandson, Boy. Papa Charles spoke on my behalf.

Glad to make your acquaintance, Roy. You like Neccos? He produced a roll of Neccos, poured them all out in his dinner-plate sized hands, picked out all the yellow ones, and reached the rest into the truck to me.

*I've just tightened down the housing on that troublesome Lateral A valve
again, Charles.*

*Thank you Bernard, Papa Charles said and flung his hands up, you stopped
my curse!*

You dropped your purse! The little lady has you carrying a purse now?

Jesus Bernard, I might as well be talkin' to your dog.

Bernard busied himself rolling a cigarette, a Tom Mix process consuming several
minutes and requiring an uncanny dexterity of both fingers and lips. When he
finished he had what looked like an old woman's pinkie and lit it with a match he
struck with his thumb nail.

*Glenda and Doris, the girls at the government yard, said that new valve seat will be
here next week.*

Bernard, Papa Charles said real loud so Bernard could hear, *is your imagination
big enough to get a fix on the boulder holder bra Glenda must wear to keep that tag
team from breaking out of the ring and terrorizing restrooms across the nation?*

The ugly stepsisters, Anastasia and Drizella. Bernard smiled at his response.

Bowling balls at the Mammary Lanes, Papa Charles began giggling.

The boobsy twins at the fat farm. Bernard was slapping his delight on the hood of
the pickup.

Godzilla and Timba. Papa Charles was getting into it.

Pluck and Moxie, Bernard added slamming his hand on the hood again.

Two run-away coal burners with their lights on.

Couple of one-eyed Sumos at the cleavage of hell.

Ike and Dick, Whitehouse boobs! Papa Charles was bumping his head on the steering wheel.

Lucky for me Oklahoma has an appointment with the vet, so I get to leave. Boy, you be stayin' here with the lecher. Bernard snorted with a gasp of air and Papa Charles reached out the window and gave him a congratulatory tap on the shoulder.

As Bernard pulled away Papa Charles was still chuckling. *That Bernard is a hoot!*

Papa Charles, what were you guys talking about?

Bowling.

I thought so.

Riding back to town that afternoon Papa Charles was telling me to learn a skill with my hands;

Your head's going to go south someday and leave your hands here to think for themselves.

As he drove that narrow levy road along the ditch, his hands illustrated their independence as they moved along with his words, as though they needed these supporting gestures to stand up and say their meaning, leaving the steering wheel to think for itself. When he was talking nobody was driving, so important were his hands to his words. It was necessary that I carry the conversation to allow his hands to settle back on the wheel and keep us out of the ditch.

Mame Ursherwood has bad breath, is what I came up with.

His hands both left the wheel to respond to my observation; *Yes, and that woman has a face that is guaranteed to bring permanent trauma to small children, with a mouth that can't quite reach its other side so has no choice but to hang open. But the heart that beats beneath is a kind one.*

We were staying out of the ditch by the grace of that truck having driven along it so many times. Papa Charles's hands weren't guiding it. I was getting nervous, *I told Mrs. Strohshiem that Carl Longernecker had been cheating by using my lunch tray to pretend like he was getting seconds because his mama didn't have any money to give him for lunch. I guess he didn't get lunch that day and I felt pretty bad and got a stomachache from eating mine and couldn't play baseball that afternoon.*

Up his hands came, *That's it Boy, you've hooked that fish!*

Patsy Coon says she can fly an airplane.

Do you believe her?

Yes.

Why?

I can drive my dad's tractor.

A tractor is different from an airplane.

I know that, I said incredulously; *Airplanes have wings.*

Besides the police won't let a ten year-old fly a plane.

Will I get arrested for driving the tractor?

No, because you only drive it at the farm.

Maybe Betty only flies her plane at her house.

Finally we were off the ditch and I fell silent out of conversation fatigue.

We stopped at Papa Charles's friend, George's gas station, and bought gas.

I'll soon be walking my ditch route, George, if you keep picking my pocket with your expensive gas.

Who's this fella you got with you? George asked ignoring Papa Charles's comment, then moving around the front of the truck to clean my side of the windshield. *This your brother, Charles?*

I am sure I rolled my eyes, a non-verbal for 'you can't be serious'. My sister taught me this; grownups can really be dumb.

He's my grandpa. I explained my eyebrows about on the top of my head.

I know who he is, so who are you?

I looked at Papa Charles hoping to get myself out of this silly conversation.

Yes, Papa Charles said, *Who are you?*

I'm Boy! was my frustrated call, both hands up in a Papa Charles's gesture to help my head out with the explanation.

You're Boy? Look how you've grown!

Whoa, George, I'll be doin' the groaning around here. Twentynine cents a gallon and you haven't even checked my oil.

You're a hard nut, Charles, but a good customer, so I'm going to offer you something free.

Last time you offered me something free, George, it was to check my brakes and it cost me fifty bucks.

If you're still interested, it is time for Mitsy to wean those pups.

Well, that's good timing, Bernard had his old dog euthanized today. Boy, why don't you run in the station there and pick out a puppy for Bernard.

I found a brown squirming pile of puppies, like somebody rolled a pair of wool socks together, growling and playing. There was Mitsy, sitting off by herself, like any single mom, staring out the window imaging how life will be when the kids are gone. Then I spotted a solitary little puddle of a puppy sitting in the opposite corner— the runt—uninvited to the wrestling match and I understood how she felt. So the choice was easy. That little girl just form-fit in my arms and when I brought her out of the station George was just slamming the massive hood on the pickup. Like a big caliber gunshot, the windows shuttered, a nearby tree quaked and the puppy flinched then settled back into the crook of my elbow.

We stopped at Bauer's Feed Store on the way to Bernard's to get a bag of Purina Puppy Chow and while Papa Charles was having a spirited and demonstrative conversation with old man Hiram Bauer, I roamed the squeaky wooden floors of the feed store, the puppy tucked in my arms. The terrestrial pleasing smell of grain and leather whisked me back to the barn on our farm and I thought of my father, how he died probably wishing he were back at the farm where he would be caught hopelessly in the current of his work. His hands would be happily engaged in their task, his mind wandering ahead to the next task. If it was true what he said that, 'a man's mind can't rest in the presence of his work' then the inversion of this formula for contentment would be that a man's hands can't rest in its absence. I missed him. I drug my free hand along sacks of corn, shiny new saddles, and scooped up fuzzy, warm chicks from under the heatlamp. I didn't realize at that time that my father's tenet that one's authenticity is validated with their hands in the dirt had infected me and I would carry it to my grave.

Why are you always making fun of Bernard and then bringing him a puppy? I asked on our way to deliver the gift.

Why, if I didn't give Bernard a hard time he'd think I didn't like him. Affection takes a different form for every relationship. Let me ask you a question. Have you missed your sister these past few weeks?

I thought about her then for the first time; she wasn't sharing a room with me, she wasn't bossing me around, and she wasn't setting a good example that I couldn't hope to compete with.

No sir, not much…well, I guess I do some; I've got no one to tease.

There you go.

I don't like it when people say, 'There you go.' What does that mean, 'there you go?' There I go where? Something else I don't like is when people say, 'That's the way the cookie crumbles.' When you're talking about cookies you should have cookies, oatmeal chocolate chip—they crumble good— so when the cookies are gone there's still another bit of crumbs to scoop off the table.

Papa Charles, somewhere along the way, had slipped on a cloak of intention, his gaze focused directly in front of him, his hands on the wheel attending to the doing of this. The momentum of his benevolence was upon him; he was in dead-center of celebrating service to a dear friend.

What did you tell that feed store man that Bernard did to his dog today?

He had Oklahoma euthanized.

YOUTHenized?

Doesn't have anything to do with youth, has to do with old age. Euthanized means he had Oklahoma put to sleep.

Put to sleep? Like taking a nap?

Oklahoma was sick and in pain so the vet gave him a shot that made him go to sleep and he'll never wake up.

Dead?

Yep.

Put to sleep, huh?

Yep.

Sounds like, 'time for your nap' to me.

That's called a colloquialism; figure of speech.

Colokeyism? Do you wake up from that?

Papa Charles laughed between his teeth. *Boy, you tickle my funny bone. There's a colloquialism.*

The puppy was waking up as we arrived at Bernard's house. I was glad because I didn't want to talk about that stuff anymore. His house was little and yellow and there was nothing outside of it but a neat lawn and a clothesline—like it was in the prairie.

Bernard was standing in the open door when we walked up. His face got all funny like he was going to cry when he saw the puppy. When I put her down on the floor she got nervous and piddled a little puddle.

Bernard slapped his leg and laughed, *It leaks!*

Papa Charles stood at the door with hands on his hips puffed up proud looking like the state of Ohio.

Thank you Charles and Boy. I think I'll call her Oklahoma.

Made sense to me.

I liked Bernard. There was no hurry-up in him and he didn't appear to have any personal agenda or standard he was applying to our times together—kind of like my faithful dog, Elmer—just happy to have someone around.

When Papa Charles had meetings to go to I would ride with Bernard and his endless rolls of Neccos.

Guess what color the first Necco is in the pack in my pocket and I'll give you the whole roll.

Well, I never did guess the right color, but I got the Neccos anyway as he would dig through to extract only the yellow ones.

You're the only Negro I know and I pretty much like you.

I'm the only cathedral with toes?

No, I said you're the only Negro I know.

Well, you are the only girl I know can huff a stone clean over the ditch.

I'm not a girl.

That long pretty hair tells me you might be a girl.

That really got to me. My hair wasn't that long, just hanging over my ears a ways. My mom usually just gave me a buzz cut, but since my dad was sick she hadn't had time. When I got home that night I snuck Lottie's kitchen scissors into the bathroom and gave myself a haircut, which made me look like a cancer patient.

I emerged from the bathroom to the nauseating smell of liver cooking which when eating, took a full bottle of ketchup to disguise the taste of.

Papa Charles said, *You get your head caught in the fan?*

Lottie went off about my using her kitchen scissors in that screeching voice that made me want to stick the scissors in my ears.

One hot afternoon I was at the ditch with Bernard. Heat wiggles were dancing all around me like worms during the rapture; the grasshoppers were rattling and jumping between the sparse vegetation that survived on that scorched road. Only the occasional gust of wind kept me from frying like an egg. Dark circles of perspiration wicked out of the armpits of Bernard's shirt and that cool, swift train of water that swept by just a few yards down off the road looked real inviting.

The grave consequences of falling in the ditch insinuated itself into the admonition directed at me each day by Papa Charles to stay clear of the water:

That bank is steep and the water is deep; you'd be gone like a dollar if you fall in there and I got a full pouch of Prince Albert in my pocket so I wouldn't be able to go in after you.

Can you pee across the ditch, Bernard? I asked as he finished his chores at the power house.

Course I can see across the ditch. I can see all the way to tomorrow. I just can't hear across the damned ditch.

No, I said can you PEE across the ditch?

Why would I if I can pee on this side?

I can pee across the ditch.

Nope.

Want to see me?

Well, it's not something I've been holdin' out for in this life, but I suspect I'm going to get to anyway.

My friend Carl and I had contests all the time. He could run faster than I, hold his breath longer, lift heavier stuff, but I could out-pee him. I could pee cursive to M in the snow, although he was ten too he couldn't even do cursive and I could pee way farther than he could, so I was pretty sure I could pee across the ditch. I prepared myself, got a good pressure built up then thrust myself forward and let her fly. The stream looked certain to pass over the ditch with dirt to spare, but the wind sprung up rustling that stream of piss and carried it back toward Bernard. He ducked away from the mist and fished his handkerchief out of his hind pocket in the same motion. When he came up he was in the throes of a full laughing fit. High pitched uncontrollable cackles, hands on his knees, his hat lying upside down on the road. He laughed like a desert dog drinks. The joy was splashing out of his action. Contagious, it got on me and I started laughing and soon was on my back on the road, doubled up like I was having an appendicitis attack. He was raising and lowering his hands like a Holy Roller on Sunday which made me laugh harder. The value of a good memory and a good laugh cannot be overestimated; you come out of one exhausted and cleansed and ready for some Neccos.

Riding with Bernard was way more relaxing than with Papa Charles. He kept his eyes on the ditch and his hands on the wheel—well except once when he started rolling a cigarette while driving.

Take the wheel, child, he demanded.

I reached over and grabbed the wheel with my left hand, scared spitless.
"I thought we were going in the ditch, Bernard. Don't make me do that again."
It wasn't the ditch I was worried about, Bernard said, *I was afraid you'd steer us off the other side and down into the Indians.*

What Indians?

Look in the trees down there off the road; see those trailer houses and all the junk cars?

Yes sir.

Indians live down there.

I thought Indians lived in teepees.

Those are the good Indians. These Indians would like to feed you to their dogs.

Nuh uhn!

Yep. There's a kill-hungry dog livin' in every one of those junk cars and the family that lives in the trailer house has had a kid every year for eight years and they still only have one kid. What's that tell ya?

Don't know. Which is always the best answer to a question if you want to get to the bottom of something quickly.

They're eatin' 'em!

Nuh uhn! Which is the best response to doubt. Bernard said no more, just left me alone with that frightful image.

I'm sorry about your dad, Bernard said.

I'm sorry about them Indian children eaten up by the dogs!

I don't think he heard me because he started talking about his new dog,
Oklahoma.

You think they youthenized my dad?

Naw, they don't do that to people, but maybe they could euthanize Charles's truck.

One Sunday Lottie sent me next door with some cookies for the neighbor, old
Mrs. Doaks.

Oh, Grandma, that old lady gives me the heebie jeebies.

You straighten up, Skippy! Her screechy voice poking pins in my eyes. *Marian
has a difficult life.*

Lottie was forever telling me to straighten up. I wasn't sure what it meant, but I
think it was a threat, like when she said, *Want me to twist your ear?*

I knew what that meant. She'd shuffle up behind me and grab an ear with her
boney fingers and try to twist it off my head while correcting my behavior.

When I crossed through the hedge to Mrs. Doak's house I saw Orvie sitting on
the porch tossing puppy nuggets to their dog, Bosco, who was catching
every one.

Orvie Handcock was Mrs. Doak's grandson and he was mean from the inside
out. My friend Carl Longernecker told me Orvie was really an orphan from
a home for experimental children in Idaho, but I doubted it because he had
crooked looking eyes just like his grandmother. What I didn't doubt was that he
was serious when he threatened to knuckle my head every time I saw him.

When he saw me coming through the hedge he shouted, *Hey, Dummy, bring me
a rock.*

Takes one to know one, Orvie.

I'm gonna knuckle your head, Dummy, if you don't bring me a rock, and don't call me Orvie anymore. Call me Cock.

Well, you can bet I did because Orvie Handcock wasn't only mean he was way older then me and big. Just his hair was bigger than me. It was sticking up everywhere. He always wore the same tshirt which would have been too small for me, so it made him look like Charles Atlas. He smelled like he wet the bed every night.

When I gave him the rock he said, Watch this. He tossed the rock to Bosco who figured it was another puppy nugget and caught it in his mouth. It clinked and rattled around on his teeth awhile then he spit it out and looked at Orvie, his head sort of cockeyed like he wanted another. Bosco was the real dummy here.

Here's some stuff, Orvie…I mean Cock, I'm supposed to give to your grandma.
I held out the cookies.

Why you tellin' me, Dummy?

I'll just set them here by the door.

I'm gonna knuckle your head.

So I opened the front door and the smell of cigarettes and urine hit me like the theater exit after a bad Adam Sandler movie. There was a little tube running across the dirty floor that I followed into the kitchen and right to Mrs. Doaks in her wheel chair where the hose continued right up her nose.

She was eating a pancake with one hand, shoveling it in. I startled her and she looked up surprised, mouth open ready for the next shovelful. She was gasping for air, probably because Orvie, I mean Cock, was standing on her hose again.

Lottie said Mrs. Doaks had emphysema. I didn't know what she had, but I know what she was: she was spooky. Her eyes were just slits, her fat skin drooping over them like melted candle wax. They were creepy eyes; one went off in a direction she wasn't looking so one eye was on me and the other was still on her pancake.

She wore the same hideous dress she wore every day. It had ridden up her fat legs which were covered with blue crooked lines like a broken windshield. I was ready to bolt and run.

My grandma said to bring this to you.

She snuffed hard through her nose and indicated to the table with the cigarette in her other hand. I had to push the dirty dishes aside to set the cookies on the table. I fake smiled and waved to indicate I was leaving. She immediately went back to eating and as I turned I surveyed the disaster of a kitchen. Every surface was heaped with dirty dishes, empty cans, stacks of paper. And her cat, Horrid Death Dammit, was up there too.

Then I figured out the problem: Mrs. Doaks in her wheelchair couldn't see where the sink was and Orvie didn't know what it was for. When I left, Orvie was lighting matches on his pant's zipper and flicking them at Bosco. He started flicking them at me.

You're going to burn the house down, Orvie Handcock.

Don't call me Orvie or I'm gonna knuckle your head!

Shortly after that encounter Papa Charles was asking me what I wanted to do before I moved back with my mom. I told him I wanted to beat the crap out of Orvie.

Boy, you don't have to like Orvie, but you do have to be kind to him. You owe that to yourself. Getting even is like getting hurt; it prevents you from feeling good and if you aren't good to yourself how are you going to be good to your mom and Elmer? Things are tough for Orvie. Sometimes you have to come a long ways not to get to anywhere. What do you think of that?

Well, I didn't have a clue what that meant, but I told him I thought it was a boatload of crap.

You best keep that 'c' word in your pocket around your grandmother if you want to see the sunrise.

So great, now I had a pocket full of crap.

When I think back, Papa Charles was more than just a man, my grandfather, my mother's father. He was a place; a whole universe for me those weeks of my father dying. A universe of conciliation, like a Rolaid tablet, he absorbed 47% his weight in excess acid. Papa Charles, so far as I could understand, had the capacity and the patience to accept any strife my radically changing and confused existence brought to him, or for that matter Lottie's peculiarities, my mother's grief or any problem his many friends brought him.

He was a pillow on which I laid my heavy head. After my mother came to tell me my father had died and that I'd be staying with my grandparents for a while longer until she took care of matters of consequence and found a new place for us to live, Papa Charles stepped up his attention to me.

I was invited into the workshop to build a birdhouse. He taught me to play cribbage on his inlaid board, and he played catch with me even though it hurt his shoulder. He accepted everything I brought, everything I said, or didn't say. There were long periods of muddled silence when I was too numb with denial to generate any words.

As his constant companion I got to know the group at the Hop Inn, Glenda and Doris in the office at the government yard, and how to entertain myself during long afternoons at the ditch. I built endless links of horsetail weed trains, walked miles along the ditch road heaving rocks accompanied by explosion noises at the debris floating along, and laid on my back forming objects out of the puffy clouds.

It was a nameless afternoon as I sat on the ditch constructing a farm of roads, fields and buildings in the dirt. Papa Charles had parked his pickup down off the road in the usual place and had gone into the little block powerhouse. He had returned as his habits dictated and gotten into his pickup, slammed the massive door and began filling out the convoluted ledgers on his clipboard.

All time had begun to move away from me in slow motion after my father's death, so as I watched the old truck, when—with a pop and a groan it let go its grip on that slope as though pulled by a need as simple as thirst—it began an easy rolling toward the water, I could only record it as another distortion of reality.

As the truck's intention gained momentum, Papa Charles, bent over his paperwork on the seat, sat up to witness his entrance into the deep water. With what must have been a look of skeptical certainty locked across my face I moved toward the submerging truck as though drawn in by the wake of its disappearance. I watched Papa Charles turn and struggle unsuccessfully with the door then glance over his shoulder through the back window. The now yielding, but still merry, eyes rested on mine for that instant eternity before he was gone.

The truck was swallowed by the water as though a giant eraser was swept across my world. A vacancy replaced it, a depletion that drew me even deeper into the silence of an unexplored subconscious world where linear time and the keys of recollection cease like birdsong at dusk. At ten I had no reserve for an expenditure so great. I had no remedy for this deficit coming as it had on the heels of my father's death, and I fell into a profound bankruptcy so consuming that my fledgling conscious world-system shut down. I can dredge but scant recollection of this personal cataclysm so must in part fabricate my reaction of not moving, not blinking; hands hanging alien at the ends of my arms that had outgrown by four inches, the cuffs of the threadbare favorite flannel I wore everyday. Standing in stasis I stared at the serene water flowing by. Then out of some physiological demand to do something I ran along the ditch bank; action always a prescription for debt. I ran without direction, no intention, no explanation of what I had just witnessed; doubting I witnessed anything. Stopping, listening and hearing only the heaving of my breath, feeling the sting of sweat in my eyes, seeing nothing, I ran from that. With head down, the narrow two-track road along the ditch bank moved under me like a conveyor moving backwards. My feet plodded heavier with each step on the summer hardened road. I ran to escape a shadow of something that exceeded what I could comprehend, like a farmyard fowl under the shadow of a raptor, an apparition that sent shivers of innate fear through my unpracticed defenses. My lungs cried out to stop; my mind insisted I continue. Stopping would have required me to process this transaction and I had no means to do that. I had a strong attraction to the Indian trailers just below me off the bank; to seek an adult interpreter for what was happening, but Bernard's admonition holding sway, I ran regardlessly on.

A boil of dust approached, then Bernard's blue truck, small in the distance, a toy entering into my skewed and tear-blurred vision. He stopped, he later told me, far in advance and stepped out to stand hands on hips to watch me running without abeyance into him. He kneeled to accept me as I disappeared in the envelope of his arms. I collapsed into his clutch, buried my frantic face into his shoulder.

Where's your grand pappy?

I did not answer; didn't know how to answer. I wasn't crying; the tears all dammed up behind my desperation.

Bernard gripped my shoulders and gave me a shake, *Where's Charles?*

He sank!

He sank. You mean he's in the water? Damnation!

He scooped me up and into the pickup. *Get to a telephone*, he murmured to himself.

Forward, no turning on this narrow ditch road, and his questions and questions, none I could answer, only pointed ahead. At the powerhouse Bernard pulled down into the slot where Papa Charles' truck had slid off the edge of my earth 50 years ago where a chemical change began in me that etched the glass through which I've viewed the world and will view the world for the remainder of my time.

The water of only one of a thousand rivers that compose the ocean of who I am, but a river that is always represented when I scoop up a handful of that ocean.

Cecil and His Daddy

Written in:

Yakima, WA

My mother and I had decided I would rise above my circumstances. Because
she was Native American and my father was in prison, our placement had been
woven low into the social fabric of the small reservation town where we lived.
The prejudice was palpable. I had long watched my mother being treated with
disrespect. In restaurants we were the last served, white men wouldn't hold
the door for her, but had no compunction in handing out sexual innuendos
because she was a pretty young Indian woman. She was long legged. Her black
hair hung straight to her waist. She had high cheekbones, big eyes and a mouth
that was turned up at the corners so it looked like she was smiling even when
she wasn't, and she wasn't always smiling. She housed acres of sadness for
the plight of the Native American people in general, but specifically for old
bucks and squaws she worked with at the agency who were swept out of their
traditional niches by a flood of change they could neither understand
nor tolerate.

Slaukish was her family name and my grandfather was an important sub chief
of the tribe. He was very disappointed that his daughter had married a white
man and I didn't see much of him. I did however see my grandmother weekly:
Bya'na. Everyone knew her as 'Na.' My grandmother with long braids, beaded
skin dress and quiet eyes helped my mother with her work at the agency
on Fridays so I walked there after school. Never a hug from Na, she would
just instruct me, "He la ya hli li," "sit down." It was something like that, then
she would put her bony hand on my knee and look me in the eye, hard. She
then would sing a prayer chant to me that my mother said was designed for
wounded animals.

The opportunity to struggle against TWIAB, what my mother called 'the way it's always been,' came when I was 13 and progressed to the 7th grade. New school, new teachers, and kids from two off-reservation elementary schools to dilute the heavily Native population of students would allow me to be different. The greatest advantage I had in this endeavor was my light skin and hair. My father was a white man and I took after him.

My mother was on the fringes of the Native community because she married a white man and outside the white community because she was Native. It was because of this mixed genetics that she knew that my sister and I wouldn't be natural fits either, so she set a high behavioral standard for us and made academics a priority. She sat with me each evening as I did my homework and reviewed with me how to deal with negative biases she knew I was experiencing. Squaw Charlie I was named by some in the 7th grade.

"Let your peaceful actions speak for you, unlike your father," she would tell me.

My father had wrestled a gun away from a white cop who was pistol whipping an old Native man and it went off; the cop caught the bullet and my father caught the blame. He was serving his time somewhere far away, like Kansas, and I hadn't seen him in six years. I kept an eye out for male role models, but the Native men I knew were all locked in a bad attitude and tradition. The white men were ready to lie and cheat to earn a profit; there were few male teachers and they were stressed and seemed uncaring. So my mother was my father image which left me with some vacancy. I didn't know about tools and cars and I didn't know about relationships with women.

So the seventh grade was going well thanks to my mother. She counseled me with my bad temper and told me KYP, 'know your place,' which meant any place I wanted it to be. I could be who I wanted to be. I was a good student and a good athlete and had begun making friends with the outside kids.

That spring Percival Safford V—Percy he was known as—had asked me to be his table partner in our science class. We had been on the basketball team together. He was from Starner Heights where many well-to-do white families lived, off of the reservation. Our friendship was sealed one day in Mr. Harnik's science class when Percy dropped his ink pen and something splattered on my face. I thought it was ink and started freaking out. Mr. Harnik was lecturing about something and we were only two rows back so I started pawing silently at my face. Percy leaned over and whispered to me not to worry; that while he was studying last night he had spilled his lemonade and it had run into his pen. There was no ink on my face.

This tripped my funny bone and we both started laughing uncontrollably. We tried to put our hands over our mouths to stifle the giggles, but they just came out our noses along with snot. This made us laugh harder and Mr. Harnik stopped lecturing and stared at us with his hands on his hips. His face grew red, but we couldn't stop. Soon the whole class was cracking up and he pointed to the door and we stumbled out into the hall. The door slammed shut. When he stuck his head out a few minutes later to see if we'd settled down we were laying on the floor laughing so hard tears were streaming down our cheeks. This was one of those laughs that simply had to wear itself out.

"Go to the office!" he barked.

Well, that sobered us up a bit. Nobody escaped Principal Houghton's office without at least one hack. A hack from Principal Houghton had a stinging reputation, like a tetanus shot. Principal Houghton was a dried up old witch, but she had a paddle with holes in it so no air would interfere with the wood hitting your butt. Carl Sohappy told us she had you grab your ankles and then she'd run across the room for more momentum and greater power. Carl had gotten a lot of Houghton hacks because he was a Native kid and the class screw-off. Once after he had gotten hacks he took us into the boy's can and dropped his pants. Just below the bottom of his underpants the back of his legs were glowing red. She aims low so it'll hurt more, he told us.

Percy and I stopped at the bathroom to wash our faces and try to get control of ourselves before arriving at the office. Our eyes were red and puffy and there was still snot on our faces. It was going to be difficult to convincingly deny we'd been out of control.

Principal Houghton was waiting for us outside her office. Mr. Harnik had called her on the intercom and given her his story. She held the door open and without saying a word ushered us into her office. She pointed at two hard wooden chairs and we sat down. We were looking as innocent as we could, our hands in our laps and such.

"Percival!" she snapped once she had gotten into her chair behind the big, tidy desk. Her chair had a high back. It made her look little, but she gripped the arms with her bird-like claws and her knuckles stuck out all white and bony. "Why don't you tell me what happened?"

She was scowling a meaner scowl than her usual mean scowl. Nobody had ever seen her smile. Her cheeks were painted red and she had blue veins puffing up from her forehead and huge owl-like glasses that made her eyes look ridiculously small.

"Well, Principal Houghton," he started. Everybody called her Principal Houghton because we didn't know if she was Mrs. or Miss. Although it was hard to imagine she was married.

Percy told her the story of lemonade splashing out of his pen onto my face. The image struck me funny again and a splutter of laughter exploded from my clamped, closed lips. Well, that started Percy laughing and just like that we were sitting in front of the feared hell-bitch Houghton in fits.

"Chucky, you first!"

Chucky, I know that sounds silly. Chucky. But my father's older brother Willard had died just before I was born and so his name landed on the first nameless kid. That was me. I hated it. I couldn't spell Willard until I was in the second grade.

This was one of the changes my mother and I concocted for me in the seventh grade; to change my name to Charles, my middle name, and the name of both of my grandfathers. But Ruthie Portner, our seventh grade English teacher, was a friend of my mother's and she called me Chucky, like my mother always had. Well, all conditions were perfect for rapid evolution and Charles, became Chuck, became Chucky and soon that is what all my teachers were calling me.

"Chucky, you first!" Principal Houghton shouted. And I can tell you that stopped the laughing. "Take your ankles!" And she pointed to a place over by her bookshelf. She took two long steps at me. Percy later told me I had a horrible grimace on my face. When Principal Houghton got within striking range, she gave it all her focus bringing the paddle up and slamming the back of my legs. There was a loud snap and she instantly feathered the paddle off of me. Whether this produced the snap or was just for artistic affect, I don't know.

The sting came and intensified. I gave a long whistle so I wouldn't cry out. When I stopped dancing around she asked me, "Is one enough for you to remember respect?

"Yes. Ma'am."

She then turned to Percy, "I am surprised at you."

I suppose this shouldn't have surprised me that she was surprised only at Percy's behavior. I was a Native kid and it was expected I would screw up. "Your parents will hear about this and I expect you will have to answer to their disappointment. Any questions from either of you?"

"Yes, one," Percy said as he stood up. He was taller than me and way taller than Principal Houghton. "Why didn't I get a hack?" I felt a warm sense of respect wander through my body. Nobody but my mother had ever stood up for me.

"Well, Chucky's situation is disadvantaged compared to yours. You understand respect, he needs to learn it."

Percy stepped over to her bookshelf and grabbed his ankles. "If he deserves one, I deserve one!"

She gave Percy a hack, but we both agreed it was not as satisfying for her as mine had been. We had a large group of seventh grade boys gathered around us at lunch to hear all the details.

Percy lived in a three story house his great grandfather had built on a big fruit orchard in Starner Heights. They had a view of the mountains and the river. I was just Native town dog. When Percy invited me to come spend a week at his ranch and pick cherries, my mother thought it was a wonderful idea.

It was June, summer vacation had just begun and the Bing cherries were ripe. Normally orchardists weren't too keen on kids picking cherries. Cherries are delicate and must be picked with the stems still attached. But this year there was a bumper crop of Bings and the pickers from Mexico were still working in California so Percy's father was hard up for pickers.

Percy told me his mother would let us sleep in a big room on the third floor where there were two featherbeds. Forget the featherbeds my mother said; you have an opportunity to make some good money if you apply yourself. She had lined up a few other jobs for me that summer, painting fences, mowing lawns and washing cars so I could buy my own school clothes. I wasn't the biggest fan of the independent man scene, but I was just the kid and my mother was the boss.

My mother also thought this was a big deal because Percy's family was in a much different socio-economic strata than ours. My mother worked two jobs; at a second hand store and at the agency helping Native families negotiate the bureaucracy. We lived in a dumpy tar-papered house on the tough side of town. So my mother grilled me on my table manners: elbows off the table, napkin in your lap, no wiping my face on my shirtsleeve, excuse myself from the table and no burping. Burping was her pet peeve. She reminded me that a 'please' is always appreciated and a 'thank you' even more. And equally important as all the others—clear my own dishes!

It was like a prep-school entrance exam. My associating with well off-white folks was a big deal for her, but for me it would be work.

I didn't realize Percy wouldn't be picking. He was the boss's kid so he was the swamper. The swamper drives the tractor through the orchard with a trailer to collect the boxes of cherries that we peons had picked.

I was moving big aluminum ladders, getting my eyes poked by branches and lifting heavy boxes. When we broke off at the end of that first day I was dog tired and my hands and arms were stained purple clear up to my elbows. Percy was all fresh and springy and challenged me to a game of one-on-one basketball. It was the first time he had ever beaten me.

I crawled into my featherbed that evening and was asleep before I disappeared into its luxurious softness. My last thought was of being in a cloud. I woke thinking I was in a bathtub, surrounded by white, and all stiff and sore. By my calculations I had earned $11 dollars that day and I vaguely remember Percy's dad saying something about having to take some money out of our checks for taxes and special security, whatever that was. What most concerned me though was who my picking partners were.

There had been a skinny man, his tuckered-out looking wife and eight kids picking in the orchard with me. The boys all wore overalls with no shirts and no shoes and the girl had on a worn-out flower print dress. They were all dirty and needed baths and haircuts.

Percy called them Okies because they were from Oklahoma, but the license plate on their car said Arkansas. They parked that ratty old car out in the orchard with the doors all thrown open. The two littlest kids played in the car while everyone else picked cherries. The trailer they pulled was full to the top with junk like mattresses, clothes, furniture and an old, beat up motorcycle. That motorcycle really caught my attention.

I said hello to a couple of them, but they didn't respond; in fact they didn't even look at me. They were picking in the row next to mine so I heard them talking to each other. Actually they were mostly yelling and I heard the drawl of their southern accents.

"You keeds shut up and git workin'!" "Netty, git the babies sum bread." "I'm a gonna tan your hide if I cetch you hittin' your brother agin!"

They were different and I thought maybe they felt like I did because I was different.

When I got out to the orchard that next morning there was a layer of smoke laying just above the cherry trees. It felt eerie like I was in a cave. The smell of smoke was strong. The fire they'd built was still smoking; there were blankets and bedrolls strewn in, around, and under the car. They had slept the night right there. I was astounded. Soon as Mr. Okie saw me he started yelling at everyone to pick up their business and "git ta pickin.'"

As I worked I got lost in my head, as I can still do, thinking about personal heroics, superhuman athletic feats, girls and other ridiculous stuff that allowed me to ignore the monotony of picking. As I progressed down my row the oldest Okie boy—he was about my age—was progressing up his row and there we were picking right next to each other.

I watched him awhile in his bare feet and tattered britches. His picking wasn't any faster than mine. At one glance I caught him looking at me. Out of embarrassment I said hello.

"Ya wanta fight?" He shot back.

"Jesus, I just said hello!" He looked combustible, like he might ignite any moment. His eyes were squinty, yellow slits and his mouth was so pinched no lips were showing. The irascible face was framed with a belligerence of unmanaged, black hair.

He looked around to see if any of his clan was within hearing distance and said in a hushed and threatening voice, "My daddy got a gun."

Well, there we were with something in common. I had a gun too. A 20 gage shotgun my mother had bought me. She'd take me out to cornfields and wait in the car while I stomped around hoping to shoot a pheasant. She knew I'd never hit one, even if it was dumb enough to fly up in front of me. So I told the Okie about my gun and he looked at me with incredulous eyes and said, "My daddy got a real gun. A peestol!"

"What's he do with it?"

"He kill rich people!" I didn't know what to do with that information, and anyway I didn't believe it, but I'd never seen a real pistol except on television so what came out was, "Can I see it?"

"No ma'am . He'd beat me n you if he ketch me."

"You're scared."

"You wanta fight?"

"No, I was just thinking I would be scared if someone was going to beat me."

"I ain't skeerd. Come on!" His father, mother, older sister and two younger brothers were picking at the far end of a far row so we took off dashing from tree to tree like in the cartoons.

As we got near their car a host of smells reached out to greet me—campfire smoke, cooked beans, dirty clothes. I don't know, it was like I walked inside of an old house. The car was a big old thing, a Packard maybe, a huge back seat

and long hood. It was a mess. Seat covers were stained and torn, pop bottles
and clothes on the floor; it was beyond my experience. The steering wheel had
one of those buddy knobs with a naked woman set deep inside the resin. The
morning sun was catching it perfectly and that naked lady was lit up, red all
around her. It was like in the movies.

There was a little kid sleeping on the backseat naked except for a clown mask
covering his face. Another little boy was sucking his thumb and playing in the
dirt. I asked the Okie kid his name. He told me it was none of my business.
He was diving into the trailer full of junk, burrowing in like a gopher. I was
examining that old motorcycle and on the side it said: CZ 125. I didn't know
what any of that meant, but I was fascinated with the possibilities it presented
to me.

He came out holding a black revolver. He was smiling and holding it in two
hands, weighing it up and down. It was the first time I'd seen him smile and he
didn't look as sinister. I could tell that gun was a god object to him.

"Can I hold it?" I asked.

"No, Ma'am. My daddy, eed kill ya!"

"Give you two bucks."

"Show me." I dug out my wallet and gave him the dollars my mother had given
me as she dropped me off a few days ago.

"Fer just a seecont." He slipped it into my hands.

I was surprised by its mass; heavy, big and beautiful. I slipped my hand around
the handle and it felt like it lived there, felt natural. I'm telling this story from
faraway, over 50 years, and that revolver feels like it is still in my hand. It's a feel
on the short list of things that fit exceptionally well into a man's hand, naturally,
along with a fresh-laid chicken egg, a sun-warmed skipping stone and a
woman's breast. The happy I was feeling ran right up to my head and I raised
the gun up with a straight arm and sighted down the long barrel…

"Gimme that!" The Okie kid grabbed it out of my hands. "There bullets in eet!"

He tunneled back in to replace the gun and took off to his work before his daddy saw him. He said only one more thing to me that whole day: "You tell enybody bout that gun I'ma gonna beat the shit outta ya!"

Percy told me that night that the Okies come every year to pick—not the same ones, but always rough. Genetically redispositioned, is what his father called them. His older brother, Harrison, called them white trash.

Percy liked the Mexicans better, maybe because he didn't know what they were talking about. They had taught him a few words in Spanish last year, but he suspected these words meant something different from what they told him. 'Besame cola,' they told him was a more authentic way of saying, 'gracias'. Percy asked Mrs. Eldfield, the Spanish teacher, and she told him it meant, 'kiss my ass!'

The third day in the orchard I was getting faster and more daring in stretching for hard-to-reach cherries. The Okie kid's older sister and I ended up picking in adjacent trees. She was pretty and not as dirty as the others. I watched her as she bent to pour her bucket of cherries into the box and her floppy old dress sagged and I saw her breasts. She wasn't wearing a bra and it was like some nuclear fission thing happened in my brain. I don't know, maybe it was some perfect storm where the seas of testosterone crashed against the rocky shores of human nature, but that snapshot is etched on my retina and I can still see it and it still zings me like nuclear.

She looked up at me and said confidently, "Why you pickin'?"

She had thirsty eyes and it took me a while to come up with a response. When I did it was simple and true,"Money."

"You ain't the owner's keed?"

"Nope." Her countenance shifted a shade toward acceptance I thought.

"Most folks around her got money, ain't they?"

"Got money. You mean are they rich?"

"Ya, got cars n white houses."

"Not rich," I explained, "but got cars. I'm going to get a car when I'm 16."

"I'm 17 and I ain't got nuttin'. But I'm lookin' for a job somewheres to git away from this shittin' family. Cane you git me a job?"

"Well, no, I don't know. I'll ask my mom if she knows some place."

"You gonna tell her I'm some dirty hillbilly ain't ya?"

"No."

"That's what y'all think ain't it?"

"No."

"What y'all think bout us?"

"I don't know—different?"

"Different bad, right? Stupid poor people."

"No, I don't think that. What do you think of me?"

"You a spoiled little white keed that goes ta school and gotta television."

"That makes me bad?" I flared my eye brows and pleaded with my hands.

"No, not bad. Lucky."

"I'm not a white kid either, I'm Native American."

"What's that?"

"You know, I'm an Indian."

"Ick. But you don't look like no Injun."

"My mother is a full blood."

"Well then you ain't no better n we is!"

" I'm not better than anybody. What's your name?" I asked hoping to get away from this topic.

"Netty."

"What's your brother's name?"

"Got five, wheech one?"

"Biggest. How old is he?"

"His name Cecil. He thirdeen n mean from the git go, just like our daddy. Ain't much good in that keed. Now you tell me the name of that boy drivin' the tractor. Why he drivin' the tractor an you just pickin?"

"Percy."

"Percy? He the owner's keed?"

"Yep."

"He rich?"

"Well, that big house is his."
"All I gotta do is git a baby from him and I'm a sippin' honey."

I was only 13 so I didn't see all the scenarios real quick, but I understood right off what her motive was. Shorty, the guy who lived across the alley from my grandmother's place, told me once that a woman was like a rocky road. You don't gotta drive it many times before it'll shake your nuts loose and your car will be driving wobbly.

"Where do you live?" I asked her trying to keep her standing at the base of my ladder.

"Alabama, and it's a shittin' place and I ain't goin' back there." She was resting her foot on the bottom rung of my ladder and we were settling into this conversation real nice. "What's your daddy do?"

"He's in prison." Usually I tiptoe around that question, but here she was with a bad daddy so I just said it.

"Tarnation! What he do?"

"Shot somebody."

"My daddy too, only he not git caught. That make you lucky again. Your daddy gone, my daddy still tormentin' usins."

"Tell me about your daddy."

"My daddy a God man, ana scoundrel—beats my momma, beats hes keeds—but he ain't neva stealin' into my bed agin' no matter what he say bout God. Neva!"

"Netty!" We heard her mother's voice coming down the row. She appeared next to Netty looking real worried. Maybe that's just the way you look when you've got 8 kids and have a bad husband. Her legs were sticks and deep creases in her sunken face were horrifying to see. See talked to Netty in a whisper voice. "Your daddy hear you talkin' down here. He come at ya weeth a steek you don't hush up!"

Netty went back to picking and we didn't talk anymore that day.

Then about quitting time I heard a commotion at their camp. The old man is yelling at Cecil, "Go cut yoself a steek. Teach you ta be diggin' in my stuff!"

I came down from my work perch for the final time that day and headed toward the excitement when Percy came along swamping boxes. I hopped on the tractor with him and directed him to the Okie camp. When we drove into view the old man was whipping Cecil. The kids were all watching. Mrs. Okie had her hand to her mouth, her furrows deeper than ever. He threw the stick off into the orchard as soon as he saw us coming. Percy stopped the tractor there and he and Mr. Okie talked cherries. Percy told him his father said there would be only two more days of picking here, but they would start picking another orchard in about a week. Cecil was looking at me with acid eyes and Netty was watching Percy.

On the way to the house I told Percy about Netty and what she said about getting a baby. He got real interested. "You probably can't make a baby anyway." I joked.

"I got jizz. That's all you need!" He said it like he was experienced.

"Then you're in trouble!" I thought about how easily Percy was taken in by pranks at school.

"I'm not in trouble because I've got rubbers. Harrison gave them to me." Harrison was Percy's older brother.

"What's a rubber?" I asked.

"A little balloon like contraption that captures jizz. Its foolproof."

He showed me later and I thought I should have told Netty I was the owner's kid. After dinner Percy told me he was going out.

"You going out looking for Netty?" I asked with exaggerated interest.

"Maybe."

"Got your rubbies?" I asked.

"They're called rubbers!" He was laughing as he patted his pants pocket.

I was in bed when he returned, but had purposely not fallen asleep.

"Tell!" I insisted.

"Harrison says girls like it when you don't tell. If you start talking about your girls you'll be watching the drive-in movie alone."

Now I was really wishing I had been the owner's son.

Percy's grandfather, Percival Safford II, was always sitting at the breakfast table listening to radio news and drinking coffee when we came downstairs in the morning. Percy's father was Percival Safford III, and strangely enough his older brother Harrison was Percival Safford IV; that's why they called him Harrison.

Percy's grandfather would always greet us with the same question: "You boys wake up with your butts aimin' the right direction this morning?" But this morning he had a serious look etched on his old face as he began reeling off the news before we were all the way into the kitchen.

"Somebody with a gun wearing a kid's mask robbed the Donald Store last night."

The Donald Store sat down by the river just this side of the railroad tracks. It was kind of a sad old place. Some years before somebody came barreling down the hill and ran into the Donald Store porch and pushed it over about 10 feet. So now the front door didn't lineup with the porch so old man Donald had set an apple box there in front of the door to get in.

Percy's grandfather continued, "The robber shot a hole in the ceiling to get old man Donald's attention. It takes something like that I can guarantee you."

"Lock the doors. The bad men on TV have come to Starner Heights." said Percy's mother, Helen. She was funny and always nice to me. She was elegant, groomed and tended; what I recognized in women with money. What she wore in her home, however, challenged that refinement: pants, maybe just ahead of the trend for a housewife's transition out of dresses. They were Levi's, just like we wore, maybe because she had two teenage sons. And she wore white 'Chuck Taylor' canvas tennis shoes she said were Percy's Converse basketball shoes he'd outgrown. She moved swiftly and efficiently with a feminine grace. Her contradiction was wrapped in an old red apron that she wore like the name 'Chairman' on an executive's door. Helen was in charge of what went on indoors and everybody understood that.

Helen gave Percy away when she told me at breakfast that they had gone to visit his Aunt Francis last night. I looked at Percy with a condescending smile, but he didn't look up from his pancakes.

"What kind of mask was the robber wearing?" I asked Percy's grandfather.

"Radio man said it was a clown's mask, but too small to cover the whole of the man's face."

I was thinking it could have been the mask I saw Cecil's little brother wearing, but I wasn't saying anything. Cecil and his daddy and that gun—it all scared me.

Cecil came picking by me that day and I asked him if his daddy went out at night.

"Mind your own beesness!"

"My daddy used to go out at night," I told him. "He'd have a beer with his friends, go bowling—what men do around here."

"My daddy go out too. Your daddy ain't no better n my daddy!"

"Did he go out last night?"
"Yes, ma'am he sure deed."

"Why do you call me ma'am?" I asked.

"'Cause you ain't ' portent nuf ta call sir!"

"I will bet you ten bucks your daddy's pistol has an empty shell in it," I said in an important way.

"Show me your ten bucks!"

"I will bring it tomorrow; meantime you look at your daddy's pistol."

We talked a few more times during the day, always him telling me he was going to beat the shit out of me. I didn't see Netty all day, which disappointed me. I had worn a clean shirt without all that cherry juice stain on it hoping to see her. Then at the end of the day I see Netty riding with Percy on the tractor.

He went out again that night. Said he was going to see Netty for real this time. I had teased him about going to visit his Aunt Francis with rubbies in his pocket.

"They're rubbers, you dumb shit!" Is all he said.

Percy was in his bed when I woke up but I didn't get to question him because there was loud talk downstairs at the kitchen table. There had been another robbery that night, this time in the bigger town off the reservation. Same guy in a clown mask stuck up a drugstore and again had fired a shot to get the clerk's full attention. The shot broke a perfume bottle and perfume had splashed on everything, the clerk said, including the thief.

"Intrigue in Podunkville," Helen said. "Next thing you know we will be on the Edward R. Murrow show."

I was more than a little confused about telling what I knew. I didn't want that guy coming after me, so I just played it dumb.
Netty passed me getting her picking bucket that morning all smiles and sweet, but Cecil was cranky as ever. "How you know 'bout my daddy's gun havin' dat empty bullet?"

"Because someone robbed a store wearing a clown mask."

"You shut up or I'm a gonna beat the shit outta you." He stepped toward me with his usual threatening tough-guy posture. I was fearing Cecil less and less each day and with every threat to beat the shit out of me, he never acted on it.

"I'll bet you if you dig that gun out now it's going to smell like perfume!"

He took off, dashing comically from tree to tree in the direction of the car. When he came back he kicked my ladder and knocked it out from under me. I grabbed frantically to catch a branch. "You sumbitchin' siwash?"

"What's a siwash?" I yelled down at him. My cherry bucket was hanging from my harness and I could feel that familiar rise in temperature when my temper was flaring up.

"A filthy injun!"

Well, that sent me over the edge. I had some bad incidents in elementary school with my temper. Like the time I threw Jack McFarland's tennis shoes, tied together by the laces, out the second story window of our classroom because he was teasing me and dancing around whooping like a wild Indian. Trouble was, the window wasn't open. I hadn't had a temper outburst the whole of the 7th grade; part of my self-improvement plan, but my cork just popped when Cecil called me an 'injun'. I dropped the 8 feet or so to the ground landing painfully on my picking bucket. I jumped him before he could escape. I got him in a headlock and really bored down. I let him go when I saw he was crying. I felt bad and embarrassed like I always did when I lost my temper. He ran off yelling that he was going to tell his daddy.

Toward the end of the day as I came down to dump a bucket of cherries, old man Okie slipped out of the shadow of my tree. The hollow face and angry eyes I had only observed from a distance up until then sent tremors down my spine. He took a step closer to me. His arms were sinewy and his cherry stained hands looked enormous. "Best injun is a dead injun I heared say. Specially one wich a big mouth!"

The next day was Friday and the last day for the Bing cherries, but still I was thinking of ways I could get out of picking. Friday had always been my favorite day, being a student pretty much my whole 13 years and all. But now Friday had a new significance. I was tired and sore and especially I was scared. I would miss Netty, but I wasn't the rich boy she was looking for.

As it turned out I didn't pick another cherry. It was reported to us at breakfast that somebody had shot a man behind Jake's Place Tavern in town. I'd kept my secret long enough. I told Helen what I knew: about the clown mask, the spent bullet, the smelly gun and the threat made at me the day before. I told her I didn't want to go back to the orchard. She headed straight for the phone to call the police.

Running out to the cherry orchard was the bravest thing I had ever done, but I had to warn Netty. I hid behind a tree until I saw her leave the campfire and go out for a pee. I had a sister so I knew all about girls peeing. I could see squatting in the tall grass was a problem. She had to consider slope and run off, direction and getting her pants clean out of the way. I watched for a minute. She sure was pretty with that wild black hair and her little butt. I guess I got careless and moved because she looked right over at me and our eyes locked.

"Whatya doin' you sneaky little pervert? You watchin' me ain't ya! Well looky here!" She stood up and turned toward me. She was naked from her waist down to her ankles. I couldn't say anything. I just stared. I'd never seen that part of a naked woman before.

Finally I stammered that the police were coming to arrest her daddy for shooting a man and that she should come with me and hide in the house.

I introduced her to Helen and of course Helen took her in like the daughter she never had. It was like I had brought a prostitute into church. Netty went off to take a bath and Helen got her clean clothes. We stayed in the house with the doors locked. We didn't know what was going on out there in the cherry orchard, but we knew the police were coming.

Helen was in with Netty when the sheriff knocked on the door. He said the man and the biggest boy had run off and the police were out there searching for them. He said we should lock our doors and shut the blinds. They were going to alert all the neighbors about the escaped men.

"What about the little kids?" I asked.

"In our custody; they'll be in a safe warm shelter with plenty of food. We're towing the car away too. A deputy will be here on duty until we find them." Just then Netty and Helen came around the corner from the bathroom. Sheriff took one look at the pretty girl with the wild hair and asked, "You one of them people?"

"She's not!" That was Helen and there was no negotiation in her voice.

I called my mother to come get me pronto. Cecil had told his daddy that I was the snitch and I didn't know if he had revenge in his heart or he was just trying to run for his life. Either way I just wanted to go home. That threat was hanging out in my brain like a bad headache.

When my mother came and we were driving home I told her the whole story, except for the part about me beating up Cecil, and she asked me one million questions, as usual. She kept saying, "Oh, my God!" and, "Holey Moley!"

"I really like Percy's mom. She told me to call her Helen."

"That means she likes you—people do like you."

"Helen said you were about as beautiful as a woman could get. Percy's grandpa said the same thing; 'Maybe you will be her friend.'"

"Well, maybe so. Wouldn't that be something!"

As we came down toward the river we had to stop for a train; those cool long arms came down with flashing lights. It was going to be quite a wait because the train was just getting going after its stop at the Starner Switching Yards. We were waiting just about right in front of the Donald Store and I told my mom about the gunshot hole in the roof. She said, 'Holey Moley' again and then commented on how the porch didn't line up with door. The train was picking up speed and as I turned my attention back to it I saw Cecil, cross my heart and hope to die. He was standing in a boxcar just peeking out the open door.

My mouth flew open and my eyes got big and my mother asked me, "What is it?" I was about to tell her that I saw Cecil and, probably his dad, escaping on the train, but I stopped myself. I thought Cecil had enough trouble as it was. "I feel sorry for Cecil," I said.

"Were you kind to him?" She reached over and touched my cheek with the back of her fingers.

"No. He was really mean. Do you think if I knew where Cecil was I should turn him in?"

"Turn him in? Did he do something wrong?"

"No, but his daddy did!"

"Let's remember that your father found himself on the wrong side of the law, but that doesn't make you a criminal." I felt her looking at me, but I just let my gaze be intercepted by the train moving past.

"Do unto others…" My mother's priming the prompt, knowing if only to myself I would finish the rule. It had been fed to me since I was old enough to understand the words.

…as you would have them do unto you."

The Village Idiot

Written in:

Bucharest, Romania

Big Bend was a first name town. There was Wayne's Clothing, Al's Market George's Service Station and Billy's Pharmacy. When someone said they'd been to Ray's you knew they were shopping for tires or if they mentioned Cindy and Joey's it was the five and dime they spoke of. Beulah had the beauty salon, Slim the restaurant, Bix the barber shop and Bert's meant hardware. And if you mentioned Skipper everyone was fully informed as to who you were talking about and very interested in what you had to say; that Skipper of tragic circumstance.

It was 1958: my father had been dead for a year, my insane grandmother moved in with us, the Dodgers and the Giants left New York for California, and I thought all that could go wrong had already gone wrong. I was wrong.

My mother was working long hours and feeling sorry for me because my grandmother was so whacked, so she gave me a long rope to roam. Like most American small towns in the 50's Big Bend was considered absolutely safe for kids as everybody knew everybody and traffic was sparse. During my glorious summers I wandered the town shirtless and free the live-long day coming inside only when I was hungry or it got dark, and sometimes not even then.

Endless were the possibilities for fun stuff to do for 11 year olds; the limitation was imagination and with Fink and Skipper as partners imagination was not a problem. We would be at the municipal pool during the hot afternoons, playing dice baseball at Skipper's house, riding our bikes out to the gravel pit to fish for carp, running in the cool mist behind the DDT truck spraying for mosquitoes or shooting acorns from high up in the oak tree in our backyard with sling shots at Precious, Mrs. Doak's silly little dog (and Mrs. Doaks when she came out to investigate the yelping).

"I know who you are," she'd wag her finger blindly toward our yard. "Your mother will hear of this!"

But we were blessed with impunity, boys will be boys you know, anyway Mrs. Doaks—Spooky Trudy we called her—was a crank and nobody listened to her anyway. When my mother did get mad at me she'd make me go to work with her at the warehouse. Like the time Fink and I convinced Skipper to crawl into the garbage can and we rolled him down the hill where he nearly got creamed by a garbage truck crossing 4th street.

Then came the big accident. Fink dared Skipper and me to jump out of the 2nd story window of the abandoned Stanford house targeting a flimsy, rat-gnawed mattress he'd drug out of that derelict joint. Because I had been told—and still believe—it isn't good to accept dares, only to offer them, I dared Skipper to jump first and because the window only opened wide enough to slither out, Skipper dove rather than jumped and landed on his head.

Doctor Kluewinkle, Big Bend's only doctor, who proudly claimed to have produced every child in town (by which he meant delivered) and who was trained during the civil war, gave Skipper a shot of penicillin and told his parents to let him sleep it off. Skipper woke from his coma two weeks later to a new simplified world, a twitch-a-second palsy in his face, and spoke his only word as the new Skipper, "Yemp".

And so Big Bend accepted the new Skipper and invited him in. He held an honored preservation status with business owners and residents alike. Motorists would watch out for him shuffling across streets; residents would bring him out a glass of lemonade if he was loitering or taking a leak in their front yard. And about every business, except the Old Maids, would welcome him into their stores.

Skipper would drop into Dr. Kluewinkle's office about every day, mess up the neatly fanned out displays of Ladies Home Journals and Better Homes and Patios then Barbara, the receptionist, would smile and fan them out again. At

Al's Market a courtesy clerk would be assigned to accompany Skipper around the store to keep tabs on what he ate or broke, the bill happily paid by his aging parents at the end of each month.

He'd get suckers at the bank, samples at Bernice's Bakery, a buzz cut at Bix's, but Skipper's favorite stop was Beulah's Beauty Salon where he got to sit under the dryer hoods.

Skipper became our town's beloved mascot. So when the rumor spread in the neighboring town that he was the product of radioactive fallout from all the nuclear testing of the day, those folks would come to Big Bend and ask to see 'Sputnik Boy' or 'The Retard'. Local folks didn't care much for that and would give the out-of-towners the stink eye and tell them Skipper wasn't retarded, he was just head-hit.

Skipper would have looked marginally normal, just a regular awkward adolescent boy, if it weren't for his palsy and his big head. Even as a little kid he had a big head, but after the accident it seemed to be getting bigger.

It was about this time that Skipper began getting what must have been horrific ice cream headaches. We knew it wasn't epilepsy because Sissy Pister had that. It was always interesting and a great break when Sissy would have a fit and go thrashin' around, but Skipper would just flop to the ground, start rolling around with his eyes closed and put his big head in his hands. We would run like hell in all different directions to find and tell someone that Skipper was having what we thought was a multigrain.

His mother would get called and she'd come and roll him into the car and whisk him away, but he'd be back roaming the streets in no time. After about the 10th time, we learned to just leave him lay there slobbering all over the place and he would be all better and up within an hour.

Skipper continually lost his shoes because he couldn't tie them himself so his mother gave him his father's size 13 black rubber boots and from that day on you never saw him without those boots. Often you would hear him coming before you saw him, slogging along in disproportionate coordination to the movement of those enormous boots.

Fink and I hung out a lot with Skipper. He had been our friend and I guess
we felt some guilt for him bonking his head.

1959 rolled around and as big shot 6th graders we were spinning our own 45's,
listening to The Platters, Fleetwoods, Coasters, Everlys, Ventures, Miracles and
yes, because Skipper liked them, The Chipmunks. Other than the appearance
of Barbie and Hawaii becoming the 50th state the only event of consequence in
1959—ready for this—a Vatican edict forbidding Roman Catholics from voting
for Communists.

Skipper enrolled in school again—not in the 6th grade where he would have
been. But they stuck him in a miniature desk in Miss Reder's 2nd grade thinking,
I'm guessing here, that he could start learning again.

This was a disaster. He didn't learn anything, but what we learned about the new
Skipper was he had become a world class mimic. He'd hear a tune and 'Yemp' it
for hours. He could mimic gestures well too, like the wink. He would get his big
old twitching moon face all twisted up to one side, close an eye and smile. And
so he greeted women.

His greeting for men, including friends and strangers, was the Skipper salute.
As pre-adolescents we 6th grade boys gave 'the finger' (also known as the bird,
the flagpole and the bone), to each other in affection and derision, but Skipper
flipped you off to say hello.

Other practiced gestures for Skipper were the good-natured goosing and the
athletic butt slap. He appropriately reserved the goosing for his friends, but the
butt slap had a general audience and, I'm guessing again, it was exactly this that
got him pardoned from the 2nd grade. Every time Miss Reder would lean over to
help a little learner with a math problem Skipper would move in for the slap.

So Skipper's academic career was over, but he still had a life at school. He was
free to wander Big Bend and his daily route would bring him to the school at
recesses where he was welcome to join us in the play yard.
He would salute everyone, winking and butt slapping the girls and goosing
his buddies.

1960 is remembered for important names: JFK, Nikita Khrushchev, Johnny Cash, Bill Russell, Chubby Checker. But what is also memorable is our graduation to junior high school and the 7th grade.

This was no longer elementary school; this was the big time. As we drug our hands along the rows of lockers in the ancient hand-me-down halls of Big Bend Junior High School, we were still delicate pink children But we saw ourselves in different mirrors, imagined ourselves as independent and competent.

However our independence wasn't so much expressed in school, where well-muscled 9th graders with deep voices bullied us flagrantly, but during uninstitutionalized time like after school and weekends where our parents were giving us slack, allowing us to prove our maturity or to hang ourselves.

Much of this time was spent on Wascat Avenue which would have been just another boring Big Bend street except that White Bread Thompson's house, unfortunately for the surrounding neighbors' property value, was located there. A well-stocked refrigerator, a single mother at work and White Bread's desire to be liked by other human beings attracted devious and life-curious adolescents like Squeak, Fink, Sin and I…

and Skipper, who had an uncanny knack for showing up wherever the action was; and he knew there would be action on Wascat Avenue. We would smoke White Bread's mother's cigarettes and feast out of the fridge while trying to ignore White Bread's inane chatter. When he became too annoying for us to watch TV any longer, we'd threaten to leave and he would promise to do something stupid and personally dangerous to persuade us to stay—like breathing gas fumes from the lawnmower which would cause him to pass out and lay twitching on the garage floor. It was great fun.

It was this very lawnmower that White Bread started for Skipper to mow his mother's lawn and Skipper, not knowing where the yard stopped, mowed on down the sidewalk of Wascat Avenue passed 3rd and 2nd Streets where he took a left on 1st Street, the main business street of Big Bend. There's simply no telling how far he would have mowed if White Bread's mom hadn't rushed out of Bert's Hardware where she worked, to shut it off.

When she came screeching into the driveway we did what we always did when
the heat was on, ran like hell. Lucky for Skipper he was in the back seat of her
car because usually when we ran like hell he would be left to whiffle away from
the scene of the crime, his size 13 boots not moving until he took his third
step; and he would fall ungracefully to the ground in riotous laughter and shit
himself. He was a bit of a handful.

It was about this time that Skipper's mom gave him a funny looking Rolleiflex
127 camera. Skipper continued to roam Big Bend with complete freedom only
now he was taking pictures. Nick—I never knew his last name—the editor of
the Big Bend Independent, figuring he could cash in on Skippers status as the
town icon, began publishing one of Skipper's photos each week in the weekly
newspaper.

'What Is Skipper Looking At' appeared on page two and was immediately a
hit for the paper. Circulation increased even though the photos were usually
just ordinary objects. It didn't matter people were simply interested in what
Skipper was looking at. White Bread's lawnmower was one of these exposés.

Billy at the pharmacy gave Skipper a roll of 127 each Monday, only 12
exposures, so much of the time Skipper was shooting with no bullets or as
often as not double exposing because he had forgotten to wind the camera.
Billy would send the film off to be printed and we would help Skipper choose a
few photos, often dogs, that Nick would decide among for publishing in
the paper.

1961 saw President Kennedy establish the Peace Corp and Roger Maris hit
61 home runs. 'Mr. Ed' showed up in '61, and 'To Kill A Mockingbird' won
the Pulitzer Prize for Harper Lee. But more important than all of this, for
Skipper, was Patsy Cline's recording of Willie Nelson's 'Crazy'. That tune would
stop him like new brakes if he heard it wafting out of a store or car radio. He
'Yemped' the melody continually and listened to the record over and over.
'Crazy' was Skipper's theme song.

1961 was a watershed year for those of us in the 8th grade at Big Bend Junior
High School. I was still a skinny, knob-elbowed, mostly hairless little kid, but
a physical reckoning was evolving all around me. Skipper, always a big kid,
had grown into a Lenny-large galoot with a little mascara mustache and a

deepening voice. 'Yemp' became more of a hallelujah from the bass section of a gospel choir than the wimpish little nasal ricochet we had grown accustomed to.

The Mexican kids, of which there was a goodly number in our school, were falling into that incomprehensible bubbling caldron of puberty as well.

Romero Perez who came to our school in maybe the 3rd grade, without a word of English, had grown up with us; been a partner in our playground schemes and kicked our lily-white little asses at a game we were introduced to in PE called soccer.

Romero with broad shoulders and rippling pecs looked, in the 8th grade, like a grown man. He was a head higher than us, walking the old oiled floors of Big Bend Junior High School with a full-breasted 13 year-old Mexican woman on his arm.

He played center on our 8th grade basketball team. Mr. Petty would holler at the mild-mannered Romero, "Don't let those gringos into your house, Perez!" So when we'd 'go inside' on Romero a couple of things might have happened; we were hurt or embarrassed. But it was in the locker room, the real hot-house of early educational institutions, that Romero's celebrity reared its head.

We would study Romero's pubic hair with cautious glimpses, but peripheral vision has never been much good for study. There would be no crude words, towel snapping or rude yanks like met Skipper when he'd shower with us. Romero would bend your boney, unmuscled arm behind your back and ram your head into a locker for getting caught looking.

But water has a way of finding its level, if you haven't noticed, so by the time we'd reached sophomore status in high school, Romero looked middle aged, had a kid and was driving a piece-of-shit station wagon. We were all taller and heavier than he was and disappointed that he quit basketball. Actually he had quit school, and we wouldn't get the sweet revenge we wanted of punishing him for coming into the paint on us.

Skipper liked hanging with his crew, so you could expect him and his camera to attend every extracurricular event: noon dances, pep rallies, games and athletic practices, where he was the understood ball boy, manager, water boy, locker room fixture and the target of customary shenanigans.

What Skipper developed when he became a 13 year-old man-boy was, well a….sizeable…you know, a honkin' penis. So what he got besides the tugs, slaps and snaps was admiration and that resulted in Skipper getting his moniker. Everyone in our domain had one; Knuckleball, Fink, Sin, Squeak and White bread. I was 'Bub'. We began referring to him as Doodle. This drove the girls nuts, not knowing what we all understood, (maybe not Skipper) that it meant Donkey Doodle.

In 1962 we were all proud when John Glenn became the 1st American to orbit Earth, but maybe not as proud as we were scared during the Cuban Missile Crisis. It was the same year that Pope John XXIII excommunicated Fidel Castro and banned 'The Twist' from all Catholic schools…now that's pertinent stuff!

1962 was also our last year in junior high—what we liked to think of as our freshman year in high school—and a dangerously unaligned year it was. I spent a lot of my free time hanging out with my loser friends. The Skipper Doodle was a routine companion for me when I wasn't in school. He was a guaranteed 'Yemp', He couldn't divulge any secrets, except what he caught on film, and an impunity, a 'get of jail card fee card' came along with him.

An instance of this would be when my older brother, who was a junior then, went for a ride with his girlfriend Birdie Willy. He'd tell my mom that he and I were going to hang out so she would let him take the family car, rather than his ratty old Ford. We would go pick up Birdie and while they would make out, or whatever they did in the back seat, I would drive them around the city and the county. Skipper Doodle would be riding shotgun and we'd smoke cigarettes and listen to the radio and sometimes Skipper would look in the backseat to say 'Yemp' Then my brother would cuff me in the back of the head and say, "Knock it off!" Luckily it was too dark for photography.

At age 15 The Skipper Doodle was a refrigerator box in boots. He was well over six feet tall with sloped shoulders and arms that hung out at 30 degrees from his sides. He looked like a massive maypole. With that great round head, a Beatle's haircut before the Beatles, an oinker nose and the dark hole of his always-open mouth, he was a presence. He had outgrown his father's size 13's so was outfitted in new shiny, size 15 rubber boots. His headache bouts had become more frequent so it wasn't unusual at some point in the day to see Skipper rolling around on the sidewalk, head in hand.

During the days, when we were in school, this iconic galoot wandered town in a predictable pattern taking pictures of his boots, town dogs, little kids on the playground. We were frequently in these photos, but if they were incriminating they never got submitted to Nick at the newspaper.

Except for the Old Maid's, the gentle man-boy in rubber boots was accepted and welcomed wherever he galumphed in Big Bend. So when he meandered, as he did at least once a week, into the girls' dressing room at the municipal pool or the girls' locker room at the high school, he was generously ushered out by one of the mostly naked young women. So for those of us uninvited for reasons of sanity, we could only fire up our imaginations at what Skipper experienced and ask, "Hey, Dood, you get any good shots in there?" What typically followed was one of the girls coming out with his exposed film dangling from her fingertips.

South Side Grocery, or the 'Old Maid's' as it was known, was a mom and pop grocery near my house, only now it was a three evil, spinster sisters' grocery. You went in on a dare and when you came out it only counted toward your Fearless (or stupid) Factor if you had stolen something. Skipper was banned from the Old Maid's.

When you entered, the bell above the door would tinkle and the worn wood floor would creak but nobody appeared. You knew you were being appraised by six nasty, sourpuss eyes or however many could still focus past the cataracts. They weren't hoping you bought something, but hoping to catch you stealing some penny candy: fireballs, Sin Sins, jaw breakers or my personal favorite, Sour Straws. As the myth went, they could drag you through the dreaded red curtain into their living quarters and do horrible and offensive things to you.

But when The Skipper Doodle burst into the South Side Grocery they were all out there in force wielding objects close at hand: spatulas, fly swatters and once a butcher knife, in attempts to shoo him out.

Skipper, gentle and otherwise harmless, was a bull in a china closet. His arms, for whatever reason, didn't fall naturally to his sides, but came off his shoulders with a high degree of flarity, so as he bumbled down the narrow aisles of the old grocery store in his size 15 boots, his hands like whopper satellites, suspended out in space, swept the shelves clean of merchandise. The disturbance he created was a perfect distraction for those of us too traumatized to enter alone. We'd ride Skipper's wake into the store and fill our pockets.

It was the 1960', right? and there was a Beatle infestation we would never recover from. Beatle's music sang out of every juke box, car radio and record player. Mickey, George, Willie, John, Jackie and Bob Dylan were secondary citizens to the British boys, but we were so capriciously inattentive behind the social filters of our petty desperation, we would have missed the news anyway.

As sophomores we were on the outs. The upper class men got the girls because they had the cars. We were pimple-faced kids on bikes still, so our social lives were not lives at all. On Friday nights, to kill time, we would take The Skipper Doodle to the Pentecostal Church across the ditch where the Mexicans and Filipinos lived.

The Holy Rollers Church is what we called it. It was just a scrawny little white-block building sitting smack in the center of a dirt field. Skipper would throw that door open and get right involved. We would chin ourselves up on the window sills, spit on the dirty glass, rub a circle clean and bug-eye the weird scene inside.

The preacher guy in the long black dress would be throwing his hands up, grabbing his head and shouting. The folks in the congregation were on their backs kicking and screaming in tongues, 'Wabba wabba, yamma yamma.' The preacher guy, all long hair and crooked fingernails, would run out into the aisle where some parishioners were really going nuts and start interpreting their nonsense talk into Bible verse. And there's Skipper, on his back, rubber boots flailing over his head, hands all over the woman next to him and dry humping the air.

When he'd come out we would ask him if he'd gotten religion and he'd say, "Yemp" and then we would all go eat french fries. He would usually get one of his rollin' around headaches somewhere during this sequence.

It was during that year, 1963, that my tribe reached the American benchmark of independence; age 16. It was at this time that the most important test of our lives thus far had to be taken. I passed my driver's test with ease as I had been driving illegally for years, but finding a car to drive legally was an ongoing problem. I had to make ridiculous promises to my mom about social and academic improvements just to borrow her car. The car was a perfect carrot for her to use against me. A request to borrow her car went something like this:

"You going to a costume party?"

"Why?"

"You are wearing a white shirt."

"I have an interview at Al's for a courtesy clerk job."

"Well, what do you know. Think how surprised your brother will be."

"Can I use the car?"

"Why can't you ride your bike?"

"Think about it…we are only as successful as we appear. A man on a bike is not an image of success."

"'Man' may be a push. And let's not forget the job is box-boy not president."

"Courtesy clerk, not box-boy. Can I use the car?"

"Game of Scrabble, you have to earn 100 legitimate points and you get to use the car."

This was a very disappointing, but not a surprising demand. Scrabble would mean sitting for an hour, having to think, getting quizzed by mom and being intellectually humiliated.

"I understand the Burdick girl has been seen riding with you in my car?"

"Sometimes I give her a ride to the bowling alley. That's where she works. What, you have spies watching me?"

"No dear, the car is bugged. You want to talk about your girlfriend?"

"No!"

"I enjoy seeing Skipper's photographs in the paper each week. How is he doing?"

"He gets those multigrain headaches all the time now."

"Those are called migraine headaches and I am sorry to hear this."

"And his head is getting bigger."

" He was a hydrocephalus baby."

"He's got Mad Dog Disease?"

"No, dear, you are thinking of hydrophobia. That would be a great scrabble word though and quite an improvement over your three-letter words. Hydrocephalus is sometimes called 'water on the brain'. When Skipper was born his head bones were not grown together and fluid built up in his brain causing his head to swell up. When he jumped out that window he cracked those sutures on his skull and his head is swelling again. It is a very serious condition and causing him to have these terrible headaches."

And so it went. I usually learned something and it was reinforced to her how much of a dope her son was, but most importantly I got to use her car.

The highlight of my life as a sophomore was cruising the gut with my buddies in Mom's car. The only risk with this was the inevitable run-in with Eldon Bobbit.

Eldon Bobbit was the town thug. He was a life-long bully with black teeth, squinty eyes and a prison record. He drove a 15 year-old Mercury with flames and, like Eldon, it was outdated. The role he saw himself in was the terrorizer of beginning drivers in Big Bend before they became big enough and confident enough to kick his ass. He scared the bejesus out of all of us with this threats and bluster. When we saw his comical old Mercury bobbin' down the street toward us we'd divert our eyes and act busy digging for something in the glove box. To make eye contact would have him and his hoodlum hump dogs shouting obscenities out the window at you: "What ya lookin' at shithead?" Flipping a didoes and riding your ass through town leaning so far out the Mercury windows I don't know how they didn't fall out, he raged, "You wanna fight shitlog?"

Eldon Bobbit was, hands down, the master of the word shit. It adorned every sentence he ever spoke (shouted) usually multiple times and he proved very creative in its use. When he got himself real worked up you were a 'shittin shitdammit'. He would give you shit, take no shit, always ready to beat the shit out of you and when he'd start sputtering with anger and forget his little pretend hooligan pals' names he'd call them "You shit–for-brains!"

On one occasion, when I first got my license, we were dragging the gut in my mom's car and Skipper saluted Eldon's carload of goons. We had to flee for our lives in a high speed chase out of town to the river where Sin, Fink, Squeak and I bailed out and ran like hell for the woods, this being a practiced behavior. The Skipper Doodle just sat right there in my mother's car. When Eldon's Merc' skidded to a stop and his pseudo gangsters surrounded Mom's car, Eldon called Skipper a 'shitidiot.' Skipper unfolded himself from the back seat towering over the cluster of little tuffs and they realized that if they upset him he'd clean all their clocks. They turned their attention to the woods and shouted into the darkness, "Dorsey, you shitchicken; next time you shit with me don't drive your mother's shitsissy car!" He picked up a bread-loaf sized rock and prepared to smash it onto the hood. Skipper extended his tree trunk of an arm and gently lifted the rock out of Eldon's hand and took a picture of it.

After that Skipper and Eldon developed some form of friendship (I think Skipper liked riding in the Mercury). I played my get-out-of-jail-free card, compliments of the Skipper Doodle one more time.

It was the spring of our sophomore year that my mother's employer moved to another state. She considered moving too, but because my grandmother needed care she stayed in Big Bend and looked for another job. I was grateful that we didn't move, but with only my courtesy clerk money and the end of her savings things got pretty desperate; peanut butter and jelly desperate, often without the jelly.

In 1964 Che Guevara spoke at the United Nations General Assembly in New York City where an unknown terrorist fired a mortar shell at the building during the speech. This is good stuff and it wasn't lost on me. As an 11th grader, life on earth was pared down to a few basics: Money (I worked at Al's and gave all but what I needed for gas and recreation to my Mom. She had not found a job and we lived off my grandmother's Social Security pittance.) Food (Lots of bread) Shelter (It was getting shaky. The bank had begun foreclosure proceedings on our house.) Girls (I had a part-time girlfriend, but who wants to hang out with a pauper with no car?) Athletics (I played on the basketball team, but my friends, Squeak, Fink, Sin, and The Skipper Doodle, as their names imply, were either wimps, hoodlums or retarded) and Recreation (This meant beer).

The problem with beer was getting it. I worked at Al's market as a courtesy clerk, stock boy, and as the tab man of Skipper when he roamed through. I would stash 6-packs behind the dumpster and then scoop them up after work, but The Hairlip, Shorty the Snitch, and other bums (what we called homeless people, addicts and derelicts) got wise to our alcohol blueprint. So we had to find another means and in a first-name town like Big Bend the only alternative was Killer.

Killer was an enormous and unpredictable Indian drunk (we call them Native Americans now) who drove a frightening, disintegrating 1955 Oldsmobile and spent his days drinking at Dinky's Tavern on 1st Street. On weekend nights, when everybody but the losers were on dates, we would pull up out front of Dinky's and draw straws to determine who was going in to coerce Killer to buy beer.

As often as not, Killer would take our money and just blow us off, but often enough to keep us trying, he would deliver a case of beer and we would go down to river and drink ourselves stupid, laugh our asses off and drive home drunk.

Only once did I draw the short straw and here's how that went: I slithered through the front door and into the smoky darkness of Dinky's Tavern, along the wall behind the shuffleboard, like a rodent, to where Killer sat. His head was on the bar, his long hair fanned out like the delta of a river. I stooped down into the stench of cigarettes and stale beer so as not to draw attention to myself and said, "Excuse me Killer, sir, my grandmother sent me out to buy beer in which she soaks her ingrown toenails, and I forgot my ID."

He raised his big head off the beer-soaked bar a few inches, his long hair
plastered to his face and looked at me with one bloodshot eye and gave a
'Hump' of disbelief, maybe disdain. He held out his dinner-plate huge hand and
I put $5 in it. He gave his hand an emphatic little shake and I put another $5 on
the plate. Now he raised up his big square head even to mine, both angry eyes
open and bared teeth and emitted a deep growl. I think I remember a growl. I
put the rest of $20 I'd collected moments before on the pile which he crushed
in that dark leather fist and laid his head back on the bar.

I stood there hoping he'd ask me what I wanted and how much, maybe where
we were parked, but he just slumped there, possibly drowning in his beer and I
could see Willy the Bartender looking down the bar at us so I figured I'd better
skedaddle.

When I got into Fink's car everybody said, "Well?"

"Well, what?"

"Well, did you get the beer!"

"No, but he's got the money."

"Perfect, he's probably buying himself another drink with it right now!

You gotta go back in and get the beer."

"Not a chance."

"You drew the short straw, Sinkhole." This is Squeak securely tucked in the
warm back seat, Mr. Coward, between Sin and Skipper, knowing he faced no
danger.

"You ever wonder how Killer got his nickname: Killer?"

"Go get the beer. We'll wait in the alley."

In those desperate, certainly waning minutes of my life, I panicked and waved Skipper to follow me. He unfurled his corpulent bulk, said, "Yemp" and we went in. "What you doin' here Skipper?"

"We're just using the restroom, Willie," I said.

"Tell him we want our beer," I said to Skipper pointing at Killer from a safe distance. I knew Skipper didn't understand what I said, but I thought if Killer heard it he'd know what we wanted. Then I stood by the back door so I could hold the door when he brought out the beer.

It was too dark for photos so Doodle stood next to Killer until he finally raised his head off the bar and looked at the Skipper salute. Killer gave him a silly little drunk smile and then he slammed his hand down hard on the bar. "Stubbies!" He slurred.

"Now Killer, you wouldn't be buyin' for these boys would ya?"

"Heidelberg," he roared rising to his feet while supporting himself on the bar. He was huge—big as a door—bigger by far than anyone I'd ever seen before, except Skipper, or course.

"I'll mess this place up!"

Willie went right into the cold room, brought out a case of Heidelberg stubbies and handed it to Skipper.

Killer waved two fives at me and laid his head back on the bar.

It was April 17, 1964, right after the Ford Mustang (car of my dreams) was introduced, that Skipper tugged on the bank door after-hours and found it open and wandered in looking for suckers that were usually on the teller's counter. They had been put away at closing time so Skipper—I certainly hope I have this right—went looking for them in Mr. DeFruta, the bank president's, office. Apparently he found the suckers on the big black status desk that pale, squeaky Mr. DeFruta would sit behind and administer his power, making people sweat out loans necessary to repair their cars and where he told my mom he was taking our house because she couldn't make the mortgage payments.

The suckers Skipper found were Mr. DeFruta and Mr. Trik, the high school principal, having a gay little go 'round there on the big black desk.

I pieced this story together in installments from Skipper's unique communication style. When he would see either of these men he'd turn to me, his often expressionless eyes smiling, and with his big pudgy hand make the rude gesture of poking the index finger of one hand through a circle formed with the thumb and pointer finger of the other. When that week's photos had been processed, DeFruta and Trik's liaison was confirmed in Skipper's explicit exposure of the men and their intentions. I can imagine they took chase in hopes of destroying the film, but how fast can you run with your pants around your ankles?

Skipper was banished from both the bank and high school, but this was not a deterrent, his routine so ingrained. He was as welcoming to both men as he was with everyone and would give them the Skipper salute. But there was no friendliness offered in return. They watched him malevolently out the sides of their eyes, scowls fixed on their slinky and suspicious faces.

I kept that incriminating photo out of circulation waiting for the right moment when it could be best used to my advantage.

Sometime during the school day you'd see Skipper wander the halls of the high school, saluting everyone, or butt slapping, then he would go to the kitchen and get cookies. Mr. Trik would send Heidi, the old secretary, to shoo him out because If Skipper saw Mr. Trik he would make the rude hole gesture.

I recall our returning to class from the cafeteria one day and there was Skipper coming out of the girls' bathroom. Mr. Trik unfortunately saw this too and flew into a fit. "What's he doing? Get him out of here!"

"He had to go potty. You want him to piss on the floor?" That was Squeak sticking up for Skipper.

"Well, he'll need to learn the difference between a skirt and a pair of pants or he'll be getting locked up."

"Guess you'll both be gettin' locked up!" Squeak was pushing Trik's thresholds you could tell by the color of Trik's face.

"What's your name?" He took a step toward Squeak.

"Jack Benson."

"Not either, its Squeak Imberson." That was Fink making sure this tinder didn't die out.

"Shut up, Fink! Who's side are you on?"

"You get your crazy friend out of here and keep him out! I am calling his mother and the police."

"Call DeFruta while you're on the phone." This was great fun watching Squeak square off with the principal.

"You watch your tongue, Mr. Benson!" Then about 40 of us—girls and boys —escorted Skipper out with pats and salutes and 'see ya later, Doodles'!

In 1965, our last year in high school, besides Pink Floyd appearing, Bob Dylan recording, 'Like a Rolling Stone' and The Stones not getting any Satisfaction, the only event of consequence was Pope Paul VI proclaiming the Jews not collectively guilty for the crucifixion; you can see it was a slow year.

Until early September, that is. It was then that I scheduled an appointment with Mr. DeFruta at the bank. He was clearly uncomfortable. "Listen son, don't you be blaming me for your mother losing her house. This is the way of the world, you don't pay your mortgage, you get the boot."

I stood at the front of his big black desk looking down at him amazed at how small he was in the big chair. I must have held a menacing expression because he rested his hand on the phone and suggested that we could call the police if I couldn't handle this as an adult. "What is it you want to see me about? I am a busy man."

My heart was racing and it seemed like minutes passed before I held up Skipper's photo of DeFruta and Trik compromised on this very desk. Rage poured into his eyes and he made a feeble lunge at the picture, "You son of bitch, this is blackmail! Give me the picture or I call the police!"

"Call 'em, you queer. By the time they get here the picture and I are both gone and you can't prove a thing. And in case you haven't got it figured out yet, if my mother gets eviction papers the newspaper gets this photo."

I was so scared I don't remember leaving the bank, but when I got home my mouth was too dry to speak as the seriousness of what I had done began to penetrate my dizzy brain. I immediately went to the high school library and stashed the photo in the most obscure book I could find, Dante's, 'Divine Comedy' which was an epic poem that no high school kid would ever be interested in, let alone be able to read.

My brother had gone off to college and I Inherited his old clunker Ford. My mom thought that because it didn't go fast it was a safe car for her boys to drive, but it was a deathtrap. The tires were bald, the steering wheel came off with a light tug and there was a hole on the passenger side floorboard big enough for a Cocker Spaniel to fall through. (My dog Elmo had in fact fallen through it.)

Hey, Shitstupid." As you have probably guessed this is Eldon Bobbit talking. "That is one shitugly car."

He wasn't shouting as usual; in fact his tone was in some way affectionate, so I playfully told him, "It takes one to know one, Eldon."

He took a menacing step toward me and flipped me off. Skipper whipped up his salute and I gave Skipper the bird and we were all friends again.

Skipper liked cars as much as the rest of us. During our last year in high school he could be found any afternoon at Rodrigo's Service Station where kids with cars hung out talking cam shafts and rear ends.

He seemed to get his shivers from cars with fins. You remember fins; there was a brief, forgettable engineering cycle in the late 50's when fins were the design whimsy; Detroit's ichthyology period. And no car had fins like the 1957 Plymouth. Passing in the right light, a '57 Plymouth Fury evoked shark alerts as far from the coast as Kansas.

Stan Kemel had come to Big Bend as the new pharmacist at Billy's Drug Store. He was fresh out of college; a fashionable young man. He thought Big Bend had a heartbeat, but other than Velvet Salvina, the kindergarten teacher who looked the same coming as she did going, he was the only adult in town under 40. Stan was a natty dresser; a Nehru Jacket, sometimes a plaid button-down and, being a bit ahead of the curve, tight pants with a slight bell at the cuff. He also had a sleek black 1957 Plymouth Fury that was parked in the lot behind the pharmacy.

Skipper's routine took him past that parking lot twice a day and when Stan's Fury came into view Skipper would begin an internal, guttural growling, like a tomcat might employ when he sees a young, unsuspecting female tabby or when he has just been run over by a motorcycle.

Skipper would run his gooey fingers over the shiny surface and lay his always-open mouth on the window and drool. Stan gave up washing the Fury and just drove it with the stringy ropes of drivel running off every window, like it had been the target in a paintball war. It wasn't long before Stan had given up his Nehru jacket and was driving a Buick like all the other old people in Big Bend. Buicks seemed to be the choice of all officious adults in our town, and are, in fact, iconic vehicles of the elderly to this day. You see a Buick coming and you move to the side of the road because 9 times out of 10 an ancient, bony-armed old person with enormous dark glasses—maybe because they are blind—is driving with no recall as to which pedal, just out of reach of their skeletal feet, does what.

Skipper liked to ride in my old Ford; maybe it was that hole in the floor at his feet. He'd try to spit through that hole on the highway and it would blow back into his face (That Skipper was a scream to have along). Or maybe he liked that whenever the gang piled into the Ford it meant we were going somewhere off-road.

We called it 'Doozie' because it was incredibly banged-up with a huge backseat and no future. We'd use it to drive across fields and steal watermelons; once we spun didoes on the greens at the golf course (that didn't work out so well). When we let Skipper drive, it was the Doozie he drove.

Late at night we would let him drive around the empty school parking lot. I'd have my hand on the key because sooner or later he'd be heading straight for the building…that is until just touching the metal ignition would get you an E-lectric shock which was audible from the outside. This was very troublesome because starting or stopping the Doozie became a psychologically stunting anticipation of pain. I often left it running when I'd go into the Burger Basement or get a haircut, hoping someone would steal it and get the shit shocked out of them. If Skipper was around I would have him start it or turn it off because he was accustomed to sharp pain. As the Doozie got harder and harder to start, I had to get rubber handled pliers to do the job and when I went away to college I sold it to an old guy named Til, the night janitor at the grocery store. Til had a serious heart condition and I didn't tell him he would get a bracing charge off the key. I don't know how that turned out.

It was during basketball season that my mom got a job working in the office at Del's Insurance Agency. Del was a slimy guy, but Mom needed the job and was good at it. She could type several thousand words per minute while smoking a cigarette and talking on the phone. She said the foreclosure 'business' had been taken care of and that the bank president had been very helpful in keeping us in our house.

It wasn't long after, that DeFruta approached me as I was leaving the Burger Basement and suggested in a furtive manner that I get him that photo and the negative or some troubles would be coming my way—ones that I wouldn't want coming my way. During this brief conversation Skipper, who was sitting inside at a window booth, was performing the finger through the circle gesture as he watched us.

"And tell him to STOP doing that!"

I sent DeFruta what he wanted and was glad that if I was to be a blackmailer I was now, at least, an inactive one. But a valuable life lesson was learned: you can take transparency and honesty to the bank, as the expression goes, but it doesn't hurt to bring along some incriminating goods as backup.

My girlfriend and I started going steady after basketball season so I didn't spend much time with my crew. I would see Skipper riding around with Eldon, until Eldon knocked-up his girlfriend, Ursula. We called her 'Ursula the Ugly' because she was, and Eldon had to marry her.

Skipper began hanging out with his friend Washington Carver. No kidding, that was his name. He was a fat African American kid—that's not the term we used to use—a sophomore who didn't have any friends so he and Skipper used to walk around town together and eat french fries.

Washington lived across the ditch and when Skipper would go over there the little Mexican kids would get him and Washington to play goalie in their soccer games because they didn't have enough players. Skipper would be schlepping in his boots in one goal and Washington filled the other goal like a big dark cloud. It was great fun to watch. Skipper would usually have one of his headaches afterwards.

I did see the Skipper Doodle one day outside my study hall window. Heidi and Mr. Trik had just shooed him out. He was heading across the lawn by the parking lot when he crumbled like he'd been kicked in the nads. He laid there all wadded up, his head in his hands, rolling around for the rest of that period. The kids in class all watched for a while, but soon returned to writing notes, drawing pictures or napping. At the class break I went out and sat by him for a moment, pulled him onto his back and asked him, "How ya doing Doodle?" (What you always asked him).

He answered as he always answered, "Yemp."

"Sorry nobody came out to see you, Skipper." I know he didn't understand what I was saying, but it was important for me to explain. "They probably had to go to the bathroom or something."

I helped wrestle him to his feet, he gave me the salute, then wobbled and twitched off. I stood and watched him for a while feeling a sickening sadness in my gut. Squeak, Sin, Fink and the rest of us had kept moving on the Ferris wheel that was our lives, but Skipper was stuck in place like a big rock. I knew he could say nothing but 'Yemp'; couldn't solve a simple math problem or even read a stop sign, but I also knew he had feelings. On that day on the front lawn of the high school when I was the only one who came out to see how he was and he gave me one of those eerie, knowing winks and walked away into that kid-empty town, I knew he felt a great loneliness. He knew we were all spinning out of his life.

All this time, the knob on his head was getting bigger. Those of us who saw him all the time didn't notice much, but his grandmother, who didn't see him so often, once said, "Look how big Skipper is getting; if he grows into his head he's going to be a big one!"

His mom just let his hair grow like a giant clump of grass so you couldn't tell how much was hair and how much was head. By the time we were seniors, he was huge, his head was huge, and his hair was huge.

In 1966 women wore miniskirts, babies wore pampers for the first time and gas cost $.32 a gallon. The Grinch stole Christmas and cigarette packages began carrying health warnings, but the military was on my mind. There was an ugly war raging in SE Asia and I wanted no part of it, so I borrowed money to go to college. My heart wasn't in it, but I was. I seldom saw Skipper that year, but when I returned that summer to work as a grease monkey at the Chevrolet dealership in Big Bend he would occasionally stop by and if business was slow he would give me a piggyback ride to the Burger Basement and I'd buy him some french fries.

Just before I went back to school in the fall he gave me one of those kinesthetic winks and said, "Bub."

"What'd you say?"

He just smiled at me all flick-faced. "What'd you say, Doodle? You said my name, didn't you?"

I got to tell you it was eerie. All this time I'm thinking I'm talking to an empty container and suddenly I'm aware that that big old dumb crazy Skipper Doodle is not crazy. He's been knowing all along, listening and looking and living the life of the village idiot, wandering into the girls' dressing room, hearing intimate conversations of the bank president and the high school principal. I gave him an affectionate slug in that sofa-cushion chest and he gave me a hug that nearly left me lifeless.

It wasn't a month later when my mom called my dorm at school. When I returned from my Zoology lecture—by Dr. Higgenbottom, who was so boring he had introduced the practice of shouting every few sentences to keep the 400 disinterested students in his class awake—I was pretty jumpy after that. When I settled down, I called my mom back and she told me Skipper had died.